U

UNWORTHY

A Novel

Antonio Monda

*Translated from the Italian by
John Cullen*

NAN A. TALESE · DOUBLEDAY

New York · London · Toronto · Sydney · Auckland

This book is a work of fiction. Names, characters, businesses, organizations, places, events, and incidents either are the product of the author's imagination or are used fictitiously. Any resemblance to actual persons, living or dead, events, or locales is entirely coincidental.

Translation copyright © 2018 by John Cullen

All rights reserved. Published in the United States by Nan A. Talese/ Doubleday, a division of Penguin Random House LLC, New York, and distributed in Canada by Random House of Canada, a division of Penguin Random House Canada Limited, Toronto. Originally published in Italy as *L'indegno* by Arnoldo Mondadori Editore S.p.A, Milan, in 2016. Copyright © 2016 by Antonio Monda.

www.nanatalese.com

DOUBLEDAY is a registered trademark of Penguin Random House LLC. Nan A. Talese and the colophon are trademarks of Penguin Random House LLC.

Book design by Michael Collica
Jacket design by Kathleen DiGrado
Front-of-jacket photograph © Lara Wernet/
Novarc Images/Alamy Stock Photo

Grateful acknowledgment is made to Bruce Springsteen and Patti Smith for permission to reprint a lyric excerpt of "Because the Night" by Bruce Springsteen and Patti Smith. Copyright © 1978 by Bruce Springsteen (Global Music Rights). International copyright secured. All rights reserved. Reprinted by permission of Bruce Springsteen and Patti Smith.

Library of Congress Cataloging-in-Publication Data
Names: Monda, Antonio author. | Cullen, John, 1942– translator.
Title: Unworthy : a novel / Antonio Monda ;
translated from the Italian by John Cullen.
Other titles: Indegno. English
Description: First American edition. | New York :
Nan A. Talese Doubleday, 2018.
Identifiers: LCCN 2017054295 (print) | LCCN 2017057472 (ebook) |
ISBN 9780385542944 (hardcover) ISBN 9780385542951 (ebook) |
Subjects: LCSH: Priests—Fiction. | Secrets—Fiction. | GSAFD: Love stories.
Classification: LCC PQ4913.O537 (ebook) | LCC PQ4913.
O537 I5313 2018 (print) | DDC 853/.92—dc23
LC record available at https://lccn.loc.gov/2017054295

MANUFACTURED IN THE UNITED STATES OF AMERICA

1 3 5 7 9 10 8 6 4 2

First American Edition

This book is for you, Ignazio

Hear
how hard your heart beats inside me.

WISŁAWA SZYMBORSKA

UNWORTHY

I

If you ask me why, my answer is it's the only way I can be, I can't be any other.

And if you add that I'm a hypocrite and I ought to be ashamed, I'll say: I know, you're right, even if you're the real hypocrites and you don't want to look inside yourselves. I have a great, an enormous responsibility: I'm a symbol of flesh and thought, of matter and spirit. And I'm a fisher of souls, not bodies.

I'm a reference point, a glimmer of light, living testimony that humans do not prefer the darkness: I am my words and my actions.

And if I make people glad, I'm their smile: I'm the good I do, which sometimes I don't even know I've done. And I'm the bad I leave behind me, which spreads like the good, maybe even more than the good.

I am my body's waste, and I'm the reek of sulfur I smell on myself always, every minute, a stench that never goes away, not even when I bathe: I'm my clay, and I'm my spirit.

Life is choices, will, responsibility. I've known that since I was born. But it's also the desire I can't extinguish, it's my dream that comes to naught every day; it's my rage and my misery.

And it's my heart, which beats fast when my cock gets hard, and in that moment nothing else exists, nothing at all: only the body of the woman who wishes to be taken, banged, loved. Her breasts, her hips, her ass. The games and the moans. The eyes that close and tell me not to stop. And the lights of this desert, which explode when we come in the bed, on the sofa, on the floor.

This is what I am. No, don't ask me why.

And there is no morning, there's no day, there's no moment when I don't give thanks to my Creator, for life is a gift, a blessing, a miracle, and we shouldn't be ashamed of anything. And there's no morning, no day, no moment when I don't thank him for this frailty that makes me feel human, and for the joy my sin gives me. For the breasts I squeeze and suck, for the lips that seek mine and kiss me, for the curve of the hips: Only a God who loves us could have created something so beautiful. And I give thanks, yes, thanks, to our Father who is in heaven for the shame I feel each night. And for the anguish that awakens me at dawn and reminds me who I am, what I've promised, what I continue to wish for and to dream of.

I'm the absurdity of my Jewish name in my priest's habit. And I'm the miracle of that same name in this same habit.

I am Abram Singer, priest of the Holy Roman Church.

2

I never met my father, I know only that his name was Nathan and that he was an actor, or perhaps an artist. I've never been clear about that, actually.

He had the same nose as mine, long and prominent, and curly hair like mine. He lived on the streets, under the bridges, and he slept in cardboard beds, according to what my mother told me: He entered her house to steal some food, and they started to fall in love that very night, they were born for that moment.

He told beautiful stories, which was how he won her heart. I think about that every time I go up into the pulpit, because I must tell the most beautiful story of them all, about the freshwater fishermen whom a carpenter's son calls to change the world.

They look at me hopefully, admiringly, without knowing a thing about me. They look at me after I've heard them confess their sins, which are almost always laughable compared to my own. They stare into my eyes to tell me that the flesh is weak but the spirit is strong, and my words are the way to salvation: Every time you fall, you're reborn. And their faces light up in a smile when I hand them the body of Christ, who was crucified for me.

Even afterward, when they come to greet me on the parvis in front of the church, I continue to speak with passion, with the joy of one who believes that the crooked world can really be made straight, and they say thank you, Father Abram, thank you, and maybe even they find that an absurd name for a priest.

There's nothing that demonstrates solitude better than a priest's room: The musty smell, the books, the wardrobe containing not many clothes, and all of them dark. The missal, the prayer book. The photograph taken at the moment of ordination, the ordinand lying prostrate on the floor in front of the altar to receive the spirit that saves and guides.

Change it into strength, Father John used to tell me, and always look inside yourself, without fear of what you may see there: *Noli foras ire, in te ipsum redi, in interiore homine habitat veritas.* I've tried it, Father John, and I still believe it, but I can't do it. And every time I try, I behold the abyss.

In the evening, before I go to bed, they all come back to visit me, all my girls. I imagine them at the moment when they make it clear that we're about to do it, that is, at the loveliest moment.

Then I also imagine them when they look me in the eye and say, You're a priest, aren't you ashamed? Dena said it with a simple smile, but not Lisa, she says it with a caress, because she loves me as she loves her own life, and she can't accept that I'm married to a two-thousand-year-old church.

They appear while I'm saying mass, while I'm performing a baptism, while I'm uniting a couple in marriage, while I'm administering the last rites and anointing the sick. Once it happened even while the bishop was giving me instructions concerning this parish, whose congregation is shrinking: It was up to me to revive it, it was up to me to spread the Savior's word. He's a good man, the bishop. He may be the only priest I could bring myself to confess to.

I always have trouble going to sleep, and I have trouble waking up. "Then the night drags on; I am filled with restlessness until the dawn," I read in the book of Job. And I also read "My days are swifter than a weaver's shuttle; they come to an end without hope. Remember that my life is like the wind; my eye will not see happiness again." In my sleepless nights, I think back on the woman who gave birth to me; when I decided to become a priest, I thought I also understood why.

My parents' eternal love lasted a few weeks, and I am its only result. All the rest has disappeared, like the beautiful stories my father told.

I don't even know if his last name was really Singer.

My mother adopted it because she wanted to celebrate the people of the man who had made her feel like a woman. And a daughter. And a mother. And a lover. Daddy was always acting, she told me once, and I answered that we all do that. "It was his frailty that won my heart," she replied.

Who knows how she managed to bestow this name on me, who knows whom she persuaded or what her beautiful story was; but sometimes the simplest people succeed in doing the hardest things.

And she chose Abram because the moment I came into the world, she decided that she'd bring me up to sacrifice all I had for something I believed in.

If only I had the strength to do that.

When I decided to become a priest, I felt that strength, believe me, and I still feel it; I want to change this dirty world, or at least to change myself, which may be even more difficult.

3

I worked for three years on the lower tip of the island: first bringing land to where there was no land, and then building the two tallest skyscrapers in the world. And both of those jobs made me feel closer to God. I know that he's inside us and that the ultimate meaning of life is to give existence the proper form; a blue-eyed German cardinal told me so. He must have read my heart, because he said it with the implacable severity of good people.

I also know that life is a hard battle, indeed a *via crucis,* but when I was a working man, I seemed to see God in everything: In my fellow workers' eyes, filled with enthusiasm and hope. In our callused hands, which defied first the sea and then the sky. In the sweat of an entire city, which never slept, just like me. And in the moments of sudden silence a little before dawn, when I got the urge to sing and give thanks. And to pray, which is after all the same thing.

And I felt him close to me when I shared my pastrami sandwich with workers from every part of the world. And up there, on the 104th floor, in the skeleton of a skyscraper with neither walls nor windows, I could see the whole city, the Statue of Liberty, and then the ocean. We would have fun identifying the sounds, which came to us all together: the firemen's sirens as they tried to navigate their fire engines through tangles of downtown traffic, the ice-cream truck that played the same music-box jingle over and over without interruption, the helicopter that took off from the 34th-floor rooftop to fly some millionaire to his country estate.

I'd become good friends with Luis, a proud-eyed Spaniard who said that from up there, on the clearest days, he could even manage to see Europe. He wasn't joking at all, and we others would play along, staring at the horizon and arguing about whether the land we sighted was Ireland or Portugal. Luis was taller than me, and he had in his eyes the sorrow of one who has lost his happiness, but his stories were beautiful too. Once he told me that he'd worked in the movies and that there was no more delightful illusion. He'd known Rita Moreno and Marlon Brando, and he could imitate their gestures and their way of walking. He'd give you the impression that he wanted to brag about knowing them, to recall them with fascination and reverence, but then he'd conclude, "They're just a couple of stars, that's all."

On the day of his inauguration, Mayor Beame declared that at least fifty thousand people would work in those two skyscrapers, and that within a few years the buildings would be welcoming two hundred thousand visitors every day. A monument to the future, he said, a monument that nothing and no one could scratch, and which would bear witness forever to the power of the city whose mayor he had the honor to be. He thanked us all, Mayor Beame did, speaking in the same vibrant tones that he would employ before too long when begging President Ford to help the invincible city avoid bankruptcy.

4

I have a rich, a very rich uncle, my Italian mother's brother, but he didn't make his money himself, he married it. I don't judge him—me, of all people—I hear stories like his every day in the confessional. And besides, there's affection in his marriage, and sharing, and maybe even the love that's born out of loneliness. He's multitalented, my uncle Nicola, and full of rage and passion. He has multiplied Aunt Tess's money, and he's succeeded in conquering the world with an art gallery. That's his way of reacting to the indignities of life; nothing can stop him, apparently, he goes from success to success; but every time I see him, he seems unhappier than he was before.

When he heard of my decision to become a priest, he invited me to lunch. He wanted to talk to me and hear me out, as he wasn't able to believe a man could renounce everything that makes life worth living for the sake of something that doesn't exist. He found it incredible that I, at the very age when the young normally win their freedom, would choose a prison. And that I'd reject the world he'd won and instead turn back to the Middle Ages. *Medieval* was the term he always used when he talked about religion, and he used it with scorn, with spite, and with the bitterness of those who have lost something and feel an unconfessed nostalgia for it.

At lunch that day, he didn't say anything to me, and I kept quiet too. I limited myself to acting as his drinking companion, at least through the first two glasses. When we left '21,' his eyes were afloat, and the cloakroom girl had trouble getting him into his overcoat. Outside the door of the club, he hugged me hard, as if he never wanted to let go. He was unsteady on his legs and smelled of gin, but before leaving me, he whispered in my ear that my grandparents would have been proud.

Except for my mother, he's all the family I have, although there may be some cousin, or perhaps a half brother or half sister, on my father's side: Among the many mysteries of my existence is the uncertainty about how alone I am. And every mystery is a promise.

I celebrated my ordination with my seminary classmates, the bishop, and Father John, who knew me better than anyone. Dinner in the parish hall, with food prepared by the nuns: overcooked steak fillet, boiled carrots and potatoes. They had also made an apple pie, which though inedible was their pride and joy. My mother had left me alone that evening; my life had long since drifted apart from hers, and that was her way of showing me how proud she was. My aunt and uncle wanted to arrange a party, and they were miffed when I explained that from that moment on, I was in the world but not of the world. I believed those words back then, I wasn't afraid of anything, and I still want to believe them now, when I'm afraid of everything and I fall lower and lower every day.

From that evening I remember the stale air in the sacristy, where I exulted during the rite of investiture. And the cold floor where I lay prostrate before the scourged and crucified Savior, to whom I was dedicating my existence.

It was Father John who asked me to help the homeless; he wanted me to know the world in its deepest depths. He was right, as always, and his request was the greatest grace I've ever received. I responded to this gift with the happiness and anger that had led me to put on the priestly garments I'm wearing.

Every time I step into a homeless shelter, I study the faces of people who have lost everything and try to understand their stories. I try to understand whether or not there are limits to dignity, to decorum, to suffering. I try to understand whether their unhappiness is different from what surrounds me daily. In every human face, I was taught, there's the face of Christ, and that's something I strongly believe in: I can see that face among the hopeless, the treacherous, the murderous. Silence falls in the church when I say these things: I can see a distant glimmer of Christ's face even in photographs of Josef Mengele, who tortured and tormented my father's people. And in images of Joseph Stalin, who massacred my ancestors. I'm able to discern the Son of God's features in Stalin's peasant smile, and likewise in the countenance of the Cambodian leader who's decimating his countrymen, starting with the educated, even as I write.

And I've seen it in the toothless girl who gave birth here, in this center of hope and desperation, and who wanted to embrace her baby at once, though she could give it neither a father nor a roof.

And I look for my father too in all those faces; maybe it's not true that he's dead, maybe I've even met him. And I dream about talking to him, about listening to him, about looking into his eyes as he smiles at me because he's seen his own lineaments, and those of the woman he loved, in mine.

It was with a homeless woman that I first felt I wouldn't be able to keep my vow of chastity. I couldn't believe it; her arms were full of holes from shooting up drugs, and her hair was colorless. But I'd never felt such a passionate embrace, and in my excitement, I couldn't see that it was desperation.

We did it in the shower, and then in the dining hall at night. And she laughed and cried the whole time.

I remember the disconcerted expression on Father

John's face when I made my confession. The severity with which he absolved me, and then the kindness with which he put his arms around me.

And I also remember his gray face when he died a few weeks later. I felt guilty, as if I had been the cause of the aneurysm, and I wept like a baby, because once again I'd lost a father, and I realized that from that moment on, nothing and no one would stop me from going adrift.

5

Whenever they talk to me about it, I feel sick at heart. Some weep as they confess, others beg for absolution, and still others are looking for sympathy: "At the time it seemed unavoidable, Father Abram, it even seemed right, and they were just a few cells, Father, you can't tell me that's a real life."

The confessional is the world's garbage dump, and my task is to cleanse souls; not a day passes on which I fail to notice how young I am, how callow and unprepared. On which this world of filth doesn't provoke grief and rage in me. And on which I don't ask myself how it's possible that this mire can be the image and likeness of God.

But in those same moments, I also feel the relief of the good news and the pride of an ancient teaching: I'll make mistakes and commit sins again and again, but I will never stop putting on the habit of my unworthiness, because I am a disciple of Peter, the fisherman who denied his own master at the time when Christ was being arrested, tortured, and nailed to the cross. It's to people like us that he has entrusted the keys of his church.

And when they tell me about the babies they decided not to allow into the world, I talk about the gift of life, the only gift superior to freedom, and I make them understand that what they've done is a serious sin, a very serious sin. I try to say it with love, with affection, with respect, and I remind them again and again that God doesn't abandon anybody, because someday I'd like someone to say that to Lisa and me, who have done the same thing.

After prayers were over this evening, I felt an urge to call her, to kiss her belly, as I did when she told me she was pregnant. And then to lay my head on her bosom and weep, as I did the night after she had the abortion. She'd been the one who proposed it—I didn't have the courage—but I hadn't done anything to stop her, except for shedding a few cowardly tears.

I don't want to raise a child by myself, Abram.

I don't want him to spend a lifetime feeling like the child of a sin and a failure.

And I will never agree to let you renounce your calling for me.

I never forget those words, and I never forget the moment of joy we shared when we first found out about the baby. Or the impudence of our joking that night. Lisa told me she felt like Lucrezia Buti. Lisa's a cultured woman, she knows much more than I do, and she's always making references to art, which she studies and loves. I didn't know who this Lucrezia was, and Lisa explained that she was the novice impregnated by Fra Filippo Lippi. I recalled, barely, that the said Lippi was a painter, so she told me that he was one of the most sublime artists of the Renaissance, and that the product of Lippi and Lucrezia's clandestine love was Filippino Lippi, a painter perhaps even greater than his father.

We never spoke of this again, because the emotion we felt vanished in the morning light; but the day when we returned home after the abortion provided me with an image that reproduced the Virgin's apparition to Saint Bernard as painted by Filippino. Any woman can be Mary, it said to me, and any man can be a saint. I cried all night long, and then the next day I celebrated mass with shame and horror, thinking that the miracle of the body and blood was nonetheless taking place in my hands, and that the world is never ready for the birth of a child.

6

Don't think that I've had very many girls. After the one in the homeless shelter—I never knew her name, and I hope she's forgotten mine—there was just Dena before Lisa. We had only three meetings, and I remember every moment, every smile, every time she undressed in my presence and looked at me with desire and contempt. Dena knew what I like to do and why, she was acquainted with the black depths of my heart. Her sarcasm wounded me, but I accepted it entirely: That too was a way of living the cross, and I'm in no position to judge anyone.

I don't remember much talking; I don't remember confidences or endearments. It wasn't a relationship but rather a series of couplings. Dena's very beautiful, as she well knows. The first time we did it, I had the feeling she wanted to seduce me in order to show that anyone could fall, even a person who had dedicated his own existence to God. As if that was some sort of revelation.

And I banged her continually, in every possible way; I wanted to wear her out by pleasuring her. I also had something I wanted to show, namely that I was a man, at least as much of a man as any of the others. And then I felt ashamed of that too, and in my prayers I could find no words other than "My Lord, forgive me." But even as I spoke them, I remembered her amber body. She was proud of being the daughter of a mixed couple. And proud of her parents, who had taught her to smoke marijuana when she was still a little girl. They'd taken her to Washington to hear Dr. King's dream, and that evening they'd made love on the lawn where a million people had gathered. They had taken her to demonstrations every time there was a need to attest that the world had to change, beginning with attitudes toward sex and the condition of women. Dena called her parents by their first names, Winifred and Bobby, and said she'd lost contact with her father when Winifred left him for a woman. I wasn't the first priest Dena had gone to bed with, but the other one was much different. "One of those guys who plays guitar," she told me, as if that made him worth less, and she added that one evening they'd smoked grass together.

I've never felt as strong as I did on the day when I decided I wouldn't answer her calls anymore. After a few days she stopped trying to contact me, but the following Sunday she came to the church and sat in the front row. She was wearing a plain, sober dress—obviously chosen with care—and she stared at my eyes throughout the service. Only her too-bright lipstick betrayed a person unused to entering a place like that.

It was All Saints' Day, one of my favorite holy days. I delivered a resonant, impassioned sermon in which I tried to explain to the faithful the words that had changed my life and convinced me that my choice was the most beautiful, the highest, the hardest.

"Blessed are the meek, for they will inherit the land."

May there not be flesh in that promise? I raised my voice without realizing what I was doing, then lowered it and went on, almost in a whisper: Those words, may they not remind us of our cravings, of our desires, of our dreams as human creatures? Of our first horizon, before heaven?

"Blessed are the clean of heart, for they will see God." I repeated this beatitude twice, and the congregation attributed my tears to the emotion caused by the simple grandeur of our faith.

"You are the salt of the earth," I thundered, "the light of the world," and then I read all the way to the end of Jesus's sermon without sufficient courage to make any comment on it at all. "Your light must shine before others, that they may see your good deeds and glorify your heavenly Father."

I remained silent a long time, and then, leaning on the liturgy, I asked the Lord to remind me who I was and what promise I had made.

The assembly followed me with interest, with enthusiasm, because we all need saints, and the rite always redeems us; I'd understood that the first time I celebrated it. And I'd understood the opposite of what the proverb says: The robes do in fact make the priest, they're part of what he is.

It was a luminous day in November, the golden month in New York. Through the stained-glass windows came an oblique light to which I tried to give some meaning. And I looked upon the garments that covered my unworthiness. Then the bread and the wine.

The faces of the congregation, full of faith, were lifted up. Who knows how many of them had secrets they never confessed, not even to me. Dena had no such problems. She remained out there in the first row, gazing at me, following the rite as though she knew it by heart. Her lipstick set off her very white teeth, and when I finally said, "The mass is ended, go in peace," she replied: "Let us give thanks to God." Loud, so I'd hear it.

She disappeared from my life that morning, and when I saw her leave the church, I thought that sin was a kind of freedom.

7

As for my father, I've looked for him since I was a little boy, and I continue to look for him every day.

I miss his voice, which I've never heard; I miss his stories, his dreams. I miss his illusions, his weakness, his defeat. And I miss the freedom to love him and kill him. To be able to say Daddy, or rather Abba, which is how Jesus addressed his father.

Abba.

There was nothing like the tenderness of that expression to convince me that I should put on this habit. And nothing like it to make me feel that we always remain children.

Abba.

I'd like to call my father that because he was Jewish; that's what my name commemorates. I'm Abram, son of Nathan, son of who knows who. I don't even know what tribe I might belong to, Abba, I don't even know if you ever prayed to or blasphemed or ignored the Heavenly Father, that last possibility being the worst. But I know who your people are, Abba, and they're my people, my world. And what you prayed to, blasphemed, or ignored is my God.

I remember the looks I got from my seminary classmates the first time they heard my name. The Jewish priest, they called me, without malice, but there was always a bit of subtle dismay when they realized I wasn't a convert: I'd never practiced nor even known the Hebrew religion, and my name was Abram Singer because of a peculiar idea my mother had.

"It's a shtetl name," Andrew told me one day, and Andrew was indeed a saint, you could tell from the way he loved everything and still managed to give it all up.

"Only God is indispensable," he told me the evening after we met, but this was a truth I already knew, and what had taught it to me was that very term *Abba*.

On the other hand, I didn't know the term *shtetl,* but I envied how naturally and affectionately Andrew had pronounced it.

I wondered what would have become of me if my paternal grandparents had stayed in Poland. Or in Russia, or wherever they came from. I imagined them in the shtetl Andrew told me about, the small village where pairs of lovers flew over the few houses, as depicted by a painter whose work he was extremely fond of. And then the cows and goats and people in the crowded streets, the incomprehensible dialect, and on the roof of a hayloft a bearded man with wild eyes who kept playing his fiddle.

Then I wondered what would have happened if my maternal grandparents hadn't died in a car crash in Italy. My mother would never have come to this country, and she would never have known my father. I would never have entered the world, I thought. The love that led to my birth arose out of flights, persecutions, and misfortunes. And out of having lost, maybe forever, what my family had been, what I should have been.

Andrew took it upon himself to tell me about the history and traditions of my father's people. "You're our older brothers," he said, "and that's both a privilege and a responsibility." For Andrew, every act, every decision, even every quip was to be included in the overall plan of the Creator, who had loved us so much he had created us. I felt that way too, believe me, otherwise I wouldn't be wearing this habit, but Andrew managed to live his own existence without any yielding, and it was in that very rigor of his that he was able to find happiness.

"The yoke is light," he said once. "Don't be afraid." Even back then, he'd intuited my uncertainties, my anxieties, my abysses. And when I didn't seem convinced, he concluded, "We've been promised."

Before leaving for Africa, he gave me all his books. Absolute commitment to the desperate of the earth was his way of giving up even his own culture, which he considered the noblest attempt to read God's plan. "There's no act of authentic love that doesn't bring pain along with it," he told me before we said good-bye. "Think about Christ, think about his mother's labor."

And I'm afraid of pain, as I'm afraid of God. When I thought about our fate, I was instinctively moved to curse him, to curse that God to whom I'd consecrated myself, because one who loves us can't both require us to suffer and invite us to share his happiness.

Only later did I endeavor to bow my head, thinking that for one who has faith the yoke is truly light, and our greatest sin is not to trust.

I retreated to my room to read the books Andrew had given me, imagining him assisting the sick and the hungry and smiling the smile of a man who has given up everything. Who knows where he came from, my lighthearted religious brother, who knows what mysterious roads his parents had to travel to meet each other and put him in the world. Who knows how many misfortunes took place so that he could bring a little hope to the wretched in a far-off land. And who knows why it was precisely he who wanted to confront me with my history, with my roots, with the people so beloved that they were chosen and who nevertheless had failed to recognize the Messiah in whom Andrew and I believed.

I'll never be able to understand the Creator's plan, because nobody has that privilege. We see everything as in a mirror, confusedly, and sometimes I can't bring myself to close my eyes, to trust, to get down on my knees.

8

Whoever sees us from the outside has no idea of our tastes, of our pleasures, of the moments in which we live in the world. We have been charged to hate and condemn scandal but at the same time to be scandal ourselves. The world can never love us for what we are and what we represent, and we're supposed to feel blessed when we're despised and persecuted. What the world doesn't understand and cannot accept is that we're happy. That's the scandal, and it's one more reason to detest us. Our happiness is the object of derision, of contempt, and in the best-case scenario we're seen as poor, deluded folks who are to be pitied.

I remember the anger I felt on the evening after my ordination, when I was walking along Broome Street, proud of my new habit, and I heard a boy say to his friend, "I've never seen a sky pilot so young." I could barely restrain myself from assailing him and explaining what that habit meant and who was inside it, and then I thought that we're sheep in the midst of wolves, that's what we were told, and all this was vanity: I took the insult and offered it up to the Lord and to his crown of thorns.

How I'd like to have again, in this moment, the strength I had that evening; how I'd like to have it when I kiss, when I caress, when I penetrate, when I love. How I'd like to understand why the Lord wanted to create us out of mud, knowing that not even his breath of life would make us pure.

And how I'd like to understand why many of the most emotional, most thrilling moments carry the germs of sin, uncontrolled passion, and violence.

How I miss Andrew, with his fearless wisdom like a little boy's. And how I miss Father John, who seemed never to have been young. I miss our discussions about recognizing God in our weakness. We would talk late into the night, and he never failed to say to me, "There are things I don't altogether understand myself, Abram, but I bow my head." I always bow my head, Father John, even when I'm continuing to betray this meek Redeemer to whom I've dedicated my life. Even when I grow angry with him, who got nailed to a wooden cross for me.

I very much miss those shared moments, when the world disappeared and the only truth was to be found in that shabby, badly furnished parish room; even the neon light seemed warm.

One day—shortly before the end of my seminary studies—we talked at length about the violence inside us, which is only the most visible aspect of our natural wickedness, which keeps us earthbound, incapable of soaring. I was never able to accept that, which may be another reason why I became a priest. I continue, however, to tell myself that I can't accept reality, and I can't understand the ultimate meaning, the authentic essence of humanity, which I nonetheless love viscerally.

By way of reply, Father John invited me to watch a boxing match with him. It was being broadcast on television from the heart of Africa. "The fight of the century," he said, his eyes filled with passion. It seemed strange to me that a priest would follow boxing, but Father John admitted that not only did he follow it, he loved it with all his might.

"Yes, my son, it's a brutal sport but genuine, and the most ancient and natural of them all. Saint Paul even mentions it when he writes to the Corinthians," he added, and I vaguely remembered the verse.

9

He'd arranged for us to watch the fight in the little study next to the dining hall, the location of the seminary's only television set, an old and noisy appliance that showed distorted black-and-white images. Father John wasn't the only one who wanted to see the combat; we were joined by Father Harrigan, an elderly Irish priest, and Father Lowry, a man of the same age who kept himself in shape by going jogging after the morning mass: The parishioners called him "Father Olympian." Along with those two, there was Marlon, a young Jamaican seminarian, who was more than happy to find a group of boxing aficionados. At the last moment, the sisters who live with us in the parish came in carrying two bags of potato chips and placed themselves in a corner. I had the impression that they were more interested in us than in the fight, and they asked that the neon light be left on. The younger one, whose name was Beatrice, also served some warm, flat Coca-Cola, while the older nun, Lorraine, kept staring into my eyes. I've always had the impression—the fear, I should say—that she knows everything about me, and when she comes to take Communion, she brushes my hands: a caress, a warning, I don't know. And I feel naked to my innards. Father John used to say that she was the most intelligent person in the whole parish, and then he'd add: "In the etymological sense of *intus legere*." Maybe he too knew all about me.

Father John, priest and passionate boxing fan, was in his element that evening, and we were all hanging on his words. He explained that the match we were about to see was much more than a sporting event: The principals were George Foreman and Muhammad Ali, two great champions who interpreted the sport, and life itself, in opposite ways. Their contest would pit strength against intelligence, power against speed, self-sacrifice against talent. Foreman was the reigning heavyweight champion, having demolished both Joe Frazier and Ken Norton, the only two fighters who had ever managed to defeat the man who continued to define himself as "the greatest!" Nobody believed that Ali could do it: He was older and more weathered than Foreman, and the years of inactivity had weighed down his body and perhaps also his genius. Even the people in Ali's entourage were full of apprehension, and those closest to him—like Bundini Brown, the friend who had followed him into every battle—were filled with terror at the notion that nothing but his pride, which hadn't allowed him to bow his head even to the United States government, would keep him on his feet as he took a certain, devastating beating. But Ali wasn't afraid, it was one of the characteristics of his talent, and his reply to Bundini's anguished grimaces was, "Tonight we're gonna dance." And then he repeated it again and again, almost singing; it was the refrain that would break the spell. And Bundini tried to smile, but he was terrified.

Father John knew the names of all the members of Ali's entourage and enjoyed recognizing them on the screen. "That's Angelo Dundee, and that one's Ferdie Pacheco, Ali would never step into the ring without him," and just at that moment we saw Ali repeat to Ferdie, too, "Tonight we're gonna dance," smiling like a kid. Father John also said that Ali was a Black Muslim, but nobody in the room seemed to consider that a very important fact.

Even the venue was epic, he told us: That land had produced the ancestors of many past champions, maybe even the forefathers of tonight's two contestants, but now Zaire was governed by Mobutu Sese Seko, a ruthless dictator, who was hosting the event in order to project an image of power and centrality. To ensure that the live broadcast of the contest would occur at a convenient hour for American viewers, Mobutu had agreed to let the fight take place at four in the morning local time, but among the sixty thousand spectators in the stadium, there wasn't one who felt tired. And the dictator in the presidential stand displayed to the whole world his leopard-skin toque and tight-lipped smile, the smile of a man who has inflicted much pain.

When Muhammad Ali appeared on the screen, Marlon rose to his feet, started cheering, and then sat down again, daunted by his own explosion of enthusiasm. The nuns smiled, while the two old priests muttered something without joining the conversation. Father John smiled too; he loved Ali's courage, and he hoped that the night would provide a replay of the combat between David and Goliath. There was no middle ground for Ali, Father John explained: This match would either mark the end of his career or consecrate him as the greatest of all time.

Foreman was scary to behold; he was gigantic, and in his eyes no light could be seen. That was what struck fear into the hearts of Ali's seconds, his fans, and Marlon, who could hardly stay seated. I too was disturbed by Foreman's stare, which promised pain but was somehow more sincere than Ali's brazen, jokey mugging. Ali also needed to inflict damage, to wound, dominate, humiliate. I thought that David also was brazen, and that he'd done much he needed forgiveness for—we priests refer everything back to the Bible.

They stared into each other's eyes without blinking while the referee, Zack Clayton, gave them their final instructions. They didn't listen to a word he said, even though he was shouting as though he wanted to be heard by the whole world. The two fighters knew the rules by heart, and they were aware that something quite different was at stake in that moment: The man who sustained the other's glare and demonstrated his fearlessness before the promise of certain pain would win the fight.

Everyone in the stadium understood that, and so did we; in those few timeless seconds, all we could hear was silence. Then came the roar of the crowd, earsplitting, savage, exasperated: The prelude to a liturgy of triumph and death.

When Ali got to his corner to wait for the bell that would open the fight, he turned his back to his rival and began to urge on the people in the crowd, all of whom were rooting for him.

He was tall and handsome, and he had a noble body, as though he were some African prince. As soon as he raised his arms to the sky, everyone began to shout, and he shouted too, directing the crowd like an orchestra conductor while it screamed with one voice: *"Bomaye! Bomaye!"*

We couldn't understand, there in the room, under the neon lights. Not even Father John knew the meaning of the word, but then the television commentator explained that it meant "kill him," and the people were chanting it repeatedly, louder and louder.

"*Bomaye!*"
"*Bomaye!*"
"*Bomaye!*"

Boxing is that too, it's useless to deny it.

Father John said nothing, he had no need to, and he kept on staring at the black-and-white television screen, praying that it wouldn't go dark at precisely this time. We couldn't tell what color Foreman's trunks were. And Sister Lorraine stared at the screen, saddened by all that shouting for death.

When the bell rang, Foreman raced to the center of the ring and fired off two explosive, impressively powerful, straight right-hand punches; he wanted to end the fight as soon as possible, as he'd done with Frazier, who was smashed to the canvas six times in two rounds. But Ali pulled back an inch or two and managed to soften the impact of the blows. There was no other boxer capable of performing that defensive move with so much grace and speed. And he did it with the slightest of smiles on his face, because he knew he was the greatest. Then, an instant later, he threw a combination of straight rights to the face: rapid, insidious, cocky. And Foreman looked at him, dumbfounded.

"*Bomaye!*"
"*Bomaye!*"
"*Bomaye!*"

Nothing like it had ever been seen; the first round

is for study, for prudence, for defense. And Ali was smiling, answering blow for blow and dropping his guard to show he wasn't afraid, tonight he was going to dance.

Life never turns out the way we plan. I was reminded of that truth even by the brutal, animal rite—as ancient as bullying, as ancient as pain—that I was watching. The two fighters knew it too, for in that moment they went into a clinch, and then they returned to the assault, launching explosive, implacable, murderous rights and lefts.

Ali began to dance, as only he could, because he'd promised his friends and the whole world that he would; he wasn't going to wind up like Frazier and Norton, and the clumsy lout confronting him was only a usurper.

The crowd immediately understood what was going on and went wild with joy. Their shouts echoed throughout the stadium, along the Congo River, and then into the heart of the forest, louder and louder, more and more ecstatic. And that orgasmic sound reached us and reverberated in every part of the world.

"*Bomaye!*"

"*Bomaye!*"

"*Bomaye!*"

The two champions continued to strike each other, all the while staring into each other's eyes; they both knew there would be no second chance. And the delirious crowd knew it too, as did Mobutu in his leopard-skin toque and our little group, guided by Father John, in the little office next to the dining hall.

No, nothing else could exist that night, and Marlon rejoiced at every blow, because Ali had to win for him too, for his people, for whoever wouldn't bow his head and had neither talent nor hope.

But Foreman's punches packed devastating power; Ali managed to dodge them and contain them in the first two rounds, but then the pain began to make itself felt and he started to retreat toward the ropes, where Foreman subjected him to some impressive punishment. He landed long, looping body blows to his opponent's sides, his stomach, his neck, and Ali countered and gritted his teeth and pummeled Foreman's face with sudden combinations. Swift, mocking, venomous.

Beginning in the fourth round, Ali leaned back directly on the ropes, as if inviting his adversary to hit him. Foreman needed no invitation, he punched and punched, knowing that sooner or later Ali would go down. No man in the world could withstand such punches as his.

But Ali withstood them, haughtily, wrathfully, because he was born to show the whole world what he was made of, and that night would be his night.

The stadium became more silent and the blows more and more violent. Foreman wanted to smash his arrogant opponent, who showed no sign of fear;

he wanted to massacre him, the braggart who smiled right after grimacing with pain. And his punches continued to batter Ali's ribs. Foreman wanted to shatter him, pulverize him, but Ali didn't give in; the talentless oaf might have been able to destroy champions like Frazier and Norton, but not him, the greatest of all time.

The battle continued inexorably, until in the fifth round, Foreman's punches began to lose steam; he was more tired of hitting than Ali was of getting hit. And at a moment when his opponent was catching his breath, Ali unleashed a combination of lightning punches, both hard rights, that snapped Foreman's head around and made the whole stadium explode again.

"Ali, bomaye!"

"Ali, bomaye!"

"Ali, bomaye!"

Ali hit him again and again, on the throat, on the eyes, and then on the nose, and only the bell saved Foreman from greater humiliation. The reigning champion went back to his corner dazed, incredulous, enraged, while Ali turned to the crowd and led them in their ecstatic cries.

"Ali, bomaye!"

"Ali, bomaye!"

"Ali, bomaye!"

At the beginning of the sixth round, Foreman realized that the fight was refusing to follow its proper destiny and that he would have to go for broke. He recommenced punching Ali with fury, with desperation, with acrimony; no one had ever dared to treat him this way. And Ali resumed leaning back against the ropes; taking those heavy blows seemed almost to amuse him, as did showing the whole world that they didn't faze him a bit.

Again the grimaces, the smiles, the elated gestures to the crowd, while Foreman's punches steadily lost force, slowed down, became predictable, died on arrival. The poor champion, hated by everyone in the stadium, was panting, frothing, unable to believe that his punches, which had demolished every challenger, and his devastating fists, which had made all comers look ridiculous, couldn't buckle this smug, smiling clown.

And Foreman swung at him again and again, pinning him in a corner, because that was his only hope, a spot Ali couldn't get out of. But Ali was able to tie him up, to dodge or parry his blows, and to react to them with sudden, taunting punches of his own. Only impotence and frustration showed in Foreman's dead eyes, until near the end of the eighth round, momentarily discouraged, he let down his guard for a second. It was the second Ali had been waiting for, and he punished his opponent for it with the ferocity of the orca, which rips out the whale's tongue. Ali landed three consecutive rights on Foreman's face, followed them with a combination of left hooks, and watched his dazed eyes as he was spun to one side. And then he finished him with two more right-hand shots, crushing blows that sent him rolling over the canvas like a carcass that's been dead for a while.

The count was long, cruel, humiliating; Foreman listened to it, and to the roaring crowd, which continued to clamor for his death. And he couldn't raise himself from the canvas in time.

"Bomaye!"

"Bomaye!"

"Bomaye!"

That was how the fight ended, with Marlon celebrating in front of the black-and-white TV screen and Sister Lorraine closing her eyes, because the world's story is always the same. Father Harrigan had been asleep since the middle of round one, but Father Olympian was shaking his head disappointedly; he must not have been one of Ali's fans.

Father John got up from his armchair, accepted the warm Coca-Cola that Sister Beatrice offered him, and went to his room; there was no need to add any further conversation. But he was, as always, smiling at life.

10

There was a second when I was afraid I wouldn't have the strength to weep anymore.

Or to take delight in anything either. Such a state is death, I know, and I ask myself how is it possible, what have I done to become what I've become? What's happened to me?

I believe in the devil, even though I can't imagine him. And I'm sure I see him every day on the street, in church, in the mirror. I see him in the noises of this city, born to welcome and to punish, in its desperate energy, in its desolation. In the smoke that rises from its streets, in its glittering neon lights, in the sudden, unexpected whiffs of the sea. I see him in Lisa's naked body, which was created by God, who loves us both. In her perfect breasts, in her mother-of-pearl skin. And I see him in her love for me, which is as sincere as pain, and which I have condemned to incompletion.

I also believe in hell, and I can't imagine it either: a deafening silence, perhaps, and the eternal void. Sometimes I think hell is death, and only those who deserve to go there disappear forever. Or maybe not, maybe you never die and hell's the way I imagined it as a child, a place where our sinful bodies suffer grievous torments. Nothing frightens me more than solitude, and when I chose to dedicate my life to God, I believed that my defense against being alone would be to sense his presence at my side. And that my choice would give me the only strength that's of any use in this life. But the flesh is weak, Christ himself taught us that, and I wonder how often he saw it verified in his own body. No day passes when I don't think about that: When I sin, when I betray him, when I discover that my spirit isn't all that strong either.

Leave me in peace, I feel like shouting at him, leave me in peace.

And then I start arguing with him, insulting him, demanding to be sent there immediately, to this hell of his, because it can't be as bad as all that.

Especially if Lisa's there too.

There's no telling how many people I failed to save from that torment. There's no telling how many people to whose damnation I have contributed through my unworthy example. Starting with Lisa.

And I ask you why, our Father who art in heaven, whom I continue to love, even at this moment. Why?

A father must help his son. He can't leave him at

the mercy of his own frailty. He must always hold him close, even when he can't go home or bow his head or accept the abyss of his own humanity. Because that is what you have asked of us, our Father who art in heaven.

Leave me in peace, leave me alone just for tonight, which is such a beautiful night.

No, I really don't know how to imagine hell, but I know that if it didn't exist, heaven wouldn't exist either.

11

I started stealing on Christmas Eve.

I stole from the offerings given by the faithful on the holiest of nights. I did it fast, I didn't want to think about it too much. For a church, Christmas Eve is also the richest night; everyone's feeling good. I figured nobody would notice.

Two hundred dollars was all I needed. I wanted to give Lisa a present, to celebrate her femininity. And then to take her out to dinner on the evening of the twenty-fifth, after having forced her to spend Christmas Eve and all of Christmas Day alone.

It was one of the few times when we showed ourselves in public together. Nobody goes out on Christmas night, or if they do, they go to a movie. In a deserted midtown restaurant I gave her a turquoise shawl—turquoise is her favorite color. She put it on at once and stroked my hand. Then she squeezed it

45

and kissed my fingers. Her eyes were full of tears. I didn't withdraw my hand when the old waiter who had taken our order shook his head. He'd seen it all before, in this defeated world.

I was barely breathing, she looked so beautiful in her turquoise shawl, and I thought that no God could be so cruel as to deprive me of what I was experiencing. At that moment I felt love for everything: for the empty restaurant, for the waiter who had grasped the whole situation, for the red, intermittently flickering neon light on the building across the street, and for the radio, which was repeatedly playing "Feliz Navidad" and "Silent Night."

I imagined her already naked, and then, after our lovemaking, with her head resting on my heart, which was still beating like mad. Everything I'd done in the past several days disappeared: the preparations for Christmas, the meditations, the confessions, the vibrant sermons I'd given, my heart moved by the age-old rite, which invokes renewal and purity and the will to change—indeed, the certainty of changing—the world. And the mystery of a God who sends his son off to be born in a stable after his parents have been refused lodging everywhere.

Maybe there's nothing sacred except for our emotions, our pleasures, I thought. And so my theft had generated a beautiful, unique moment; it was, after all, an act of love, meant to please one person alone. It was only the next morning, when I returned to my parish church, that I became aware of how good we are at telling ourselves a suitable story about our wretchedness, and I had an empty sensation, like what I feel when I think that death's not a passage to anything, it's the end of everything. Then I delivered my homily for Saint Stephen's Day and wondered how low I would continue to sink.

Since dishonoring that holy day, I've stolen again, on many more occasions—almost every Sunday. On Sunday evenings I have dinner at Lisa's, and I always bring her flowers and sweets. Lisa loves marrons glacés, and now I'm crazy about them too. In earlier days, I used to bring wine as well, but then I lost my nerve for doing that: A priest is supposed to do something quite different with wine.

Every Sunday evening, Sister Lorraine shoots me a look that makes my soul bleed; yes, she must have figured everything out. I avoid her artless eyes and say I'm going to visit my mother, and then, as soon as I've left, I think that now I've told a new fib, or rather that I'm living a lie. But later, after I've made love with Lisa, I feel fresh anger toward life and God Almighty, who would take away from me the joy of being inside her.

12

I hear it night and day, whenever I don't want to think. And whenever I think.

Everyone who works on the church premises laughs about it; it's my obsession, they say. Sister Beatrice badgers me, shaking her head at the lyrics, which she deems inappropriate for a priest. She's a witty, indulgent woman, and she says I'm just young, a child of my time. But we're the same age.

Another one who laughs is Raj, the Indian boy who comes in to help when we're preparing meals for the homeless. He's faster than anyone when it comes to dressing the sandwiches, but while he's spreading the mustard, he too hums the tune under his breath. I try to give the impression that I'm captivated by the music: that liberating refrain, shouted proudly, freely; that explosive crescendo, disclosing a hint of pain.

But I'm well aware that what gets me is the text, the

words, all the words; they conquered me the first time I heard them, and they were written for me, or so I'm not ashamed to think.

Desire is hunger is the fire I breathe
Love is a banquet on which we feed

Have I always been this way, my God? But then why did I choose you? Why this habit, why this life? How I'd like to feel strong enough to control everything. How I'd like to feel again the flame that made me see that there is nothing in the world, nothing and nobody, whose life equals this one.

The way I feel when I'm in your hands
Take my hand come undercover
They can't hurt you now

I've asked myself if what I feel for Lisa is love, my God. I ask you too, Jesus, you who were a man, you who made yourself flesh and therefore corrupt, you who died in the flesh.

I ask myself that every day, because I know I love you, I know I have chosen you. And then I wonder how I can love her, Lisa, if I also wanted Dena and the girl in the homeless shelter. What is desire without love?

Love is an angel disguised as lust

My God, how alone I am. I know you're speaking to me even now, I know you're loving me. I know you're making me feel what it means to be human. I know you love me when I kiss her, when I come, I know you're letting me experience what my father must have experienced who knows how many times. That father of mine I never knew, who gave me life in a night of love.

Without you I cannot live
Forgive, the yearning burning
I believe it's time, too real to feel
So touch me now, touch me now, touch me now

Where are you, Lisa, when I'm hearing those words? And where are you, my child who was never born? Did you feel anything when we decided not to have you? Did you understand what was happening? What have your eyes not seen? Whom couldn't you love?

Because the night belongs to lovers . . .

I'd like to understand what love means. I'd like to understand why it's so beautiful and why it's so hard. I'd like to understand why I chose the cross, and I'd like to understand when I'll be able to feel that the yoke you've placed us under is indeed light, as you promised it would be.

Because tonight there are two lovers
If we believe in the night we trust
Because tonight there are two lovers . . .

And now what I'd like is you yourself, my Lisa. I'd like to kiss your breasts and then kiss them again.

And then to feel your beating heart and weep until morning.

13

I'm the one who says the six o'clock mass, it's a habit I've taken up since I started losing sleep. When Father John was here, I would address him during the homily. I wanted him to think me capable of spreading the good news in spite of my body's paltriness. And his rapt gaze would soothe my wounds and caress my vanity. Now I don't look at anyone, and when I happen to meet Sister Lorraine's eyes, I turn mine elsewhere.

Celebrating mass at that hour is my way of comprehending that one is reborn with each new day, and I maintain that enthusiasm throughout the early-morning hours. There's nothing more thrilling than seeing the sun begin to light up this nocturnal city, and nothing more moving than watching the first rays strike the tops of the skyscrapers. Then, inexorably, the sun is everywhere, penetrating the darkest, sorriest alleyways, and that makes me cry, My Father who art in heaven, how lovely it is to be able to thank you.

Breakfast time is wearisome for me. Every day I arrive carried away by the enthusiasm that makes the world go round. And I want to talk to the brothers who wear the same cassock as I do about how we can revolutionize this cockeyed world, about how exciting it is to love it always, even in times of pain. And about how art, even more than nature, can make us see your face. Because art is never indifferent, and even when it's extreme, even when it's shouted, it reveals that in this world, which has chosen to be the devil's territory, spirit exists, grace exists. It's the intuition that perceives the universal in the particular, as Father John used to say. Yes, those are the topics I'd like to discuss, and maybe even argue about, listening to everyone's respective, fallacious truth. Knowing that mine is the most fallacious of all.

Instead, each and every morning, we wind up talking about the boiler that's not working, or about who's hearing confessions when, or about how the offerings collected from the faithful are steadily decreasing and churches are getting emptier and emptier. People prefer darkness, Father Lowry always says.

I finish breakfast with a sense of melancholy and frustration, but then I tell myself that it's they who are right, they who are making the real revolution, accepting the boredom and the mediocrity of those conversations.

Our Father who art in heaven, you have asked us to be in the world but not of the world; but then you want us humble, insignificant, defeated. You wanted warriors like Saint Paul and Saint Ignatius, you exalted them and allowed them to enrich your church. But you continually remind us that the blessed ones are the poor in spirit, and the last shall be first. Our Father, if I didn't love you, I would hate you deeply, and maybe sometimes I do, because I know you love me even at such moments.

Father who sacrificed your son, Father who made yourself flesh and felt all that flesh desires and demands.

Father of sinners and murderers. Father of failures and traitors.

Father of my father, whom you saw making love to my mother and conceiving this unworthy body of mine. Have pity on my rage, which is like a fallen angel's.

14

The priest appointed to succeed Father John is named Jorge, and he was born in Córdoba, Spain. There was a moment when it seemed that the successor might be me, but then they must have thought I'm too young, or maybe they know what I am, and a person like me isn't the ideal model for a retriever of lost sheep.

But Jorge—he doesn't want to be called "Father"—isn't exactly an exemplary priest; in a world that loves the night, even the shepherds are weak. Our new pastor drinks a lot, too much, to the point that when he goes out to the altar, I'm afraid of what effect the wine, which in his hands becomes the blood of Christ, may have on him.

Once a woman parishioner complained to me that the pastor's breath smelled like wine, and I didn't know what to tell her. I stammered that it wasn't true, that he said a lot of masses so maybe that was why he had wine on his breath, and that in any case we must never judge our fellows. On another occasion, I saw Sister Lorraine putting water in the wine we drank at dinner. Jorge noticed this too and scolded her, but then I heard him crying later.

He's a reserved man, a man of few words; as far as he's concerned, deeds alone count. As a boy in Spain, he accidentally killed a young friend while they were playing at bullfighting. Until that day, Jorge had wanted to be a matador when he grew up. He'd play the bullfighter for hours and hours every day after school—fantasizing in his own way about achieving glory in the *plaza de toros*—and invite his companion, who played the bull, to gore a red cloth. But that day his friend moved his neck suddenly in a real effort to gore the silent torero, and Jorge, holding concealed under the cloth a sword bought at a market stall, cleanly severed the other boy's jugular. He fell to the ground, his eyes bulging as his blood spurted everywhere, and Jorge watched in anguish as life abandoned the kid, who loved bullfighting too, just like him.

The boy's mother died of a broken heart, and Jorge's decision to become a priest came shortly thereafter. Apparently Jorge was the name of the friend he'd killed; nobody knows what his real name is. I always wonder whether such decisions aren't merely emotional, but I regret that kind of speculation right away. In this area too, I'm no one to judge, and besides, what do we know about the ways of grace and how it acts upon us?

One morning Jorge asked me to accompany him on a visit to a center for handicapped children abandoned by their parents, one of the most colorful places in New York; whoever runs it has chosen this means of assuaging the outrage of unhappiness in such defenseless children. Every day, Jorge visits a little Ecuadorean girl suffering from cerebral palsy. Blanca—that's her name—has been bedridden since she was born; she's very thin, practically a skeleton, and she's got a tube up her nose.

As soon as he enters the room, Jorge kisses her on the forehead and then whispers something in her ear, maybe always the same words. Blanca looks at him with wide-open, enormous, astonished eyes. No telling how much of the ritual she understands, and no telling what she might think about my presence behind her friend, who—having spoken the ritual words—keeps her company in silence.

We stayed with Blanca more than an hour, and then Jorge suggested we go back to the church on foot through Central Park. And while we were skirting the lake, he asked me to offer up a prayer of thanksgiving to the Lord. I complied joyfully, passionately, enthusiastically, looking at the skyscrapers whose mighty presence defied the spring in the park.

He really doesn't speak much, Jorge doesn't, when he's not praying.

That evening I told Lisa the story of my adventure. She laid her head on my chest over my heart and remained still, listening to it beating with distress and desire.

15

It was that same night when I noticed a lump in her left breast.

It was a Tuesday, I remember it well, another night when I'd announced that I would sleep at my mother's. "She's going through a difficult period," I'd added; once you start to lie, you lose all sense of shame about anything.

Nobody made a comment, and I saw in their indifference the cruelest of judgments. But by then I was used to it: I would go out in silence and return at dawn to say mass. To get back inside, I'd have to make my way through a group of homeless people who were waiting for Raj's sandwiches. I'd wonder what they thought of me; maybe they had figured me out too.

I noticed the lump when I was just about to leave—I always like to squeeze her and caress her, especially when she's sleeping. Sometimes she smiles at me in her sleep, and I feel that this love really exists.

I squeezed her breast hard; I was surprised at first, then shaken, then terrified, cursing my fingers for what they were touching, and then I squeezed again and hurt her. Lisa woke up with a start, and I asked her if she'd ever noticed that little ball of flesh on the underside of her breast.

She shook her head to calm me down. It's nothing, she said, women often get little things like this, it's just your guilty feelings, Abram. Then she asked me to let her sleep some more, but I didn't leave until she promised me she'd get examined by a doctor. "Of course I will," she told me, "of course I will, but now let me rest, Abram, don't you have a mass to say?"

She wasn't trying to offend me, she actually was tired, and when I got to the door she called me back and clasped my fingers in her own. "You're a beautiful man," she said, and she smiled.

And I said my mass, because that's what we're all called to do, including those who don't wear the habit I wear. And I tried to understand how the Lord was speaking to me that day, wondering if I'd ever truly listened to him. And why we're afraid of happiness.

I asked the Epistle to the Romans, the responsorial psalm, the Gospel of Saint John. I asked the drowsy eyes of the old priests and the serene gaze Sister Lorraine gave me, along with the usual caress when she came up to take Communion. I even asked Sister

Beatrice's eyes, but she was absorbed in her singsong praying. Perhaps the most courageous deed of all is to accept your own mediocrity.

Then I tried to hear the Lord's voice in the stories the people making their confessions told me. Every man has a secret, an abyss, a dark side. I'm not alone, I told myself, but none of those others has made my choice, not one has promised to be a shepherd and to bring the good news.

I tried to hear the Lord's voice, to see his face, in the people who asked Raj for a little more mustard, and in the way Jorge led the evening prayers; only one day had passed since we'd visited Blanca, and already I was thinking about other things. I wondered what remains of our feelings, of what moves us, of the moments when we feel ready to change the world. And then I tried to hear the voice of God even in my own weaknesses, because he wanted me to have them even before I came into the world.

And I celebrated my mass every minute of the day, including when Lisa told me that the doctor had sent her to have a biopsy: Physicians in this country are all very scrupulous, there's no reason to get upset. Then, that evening, I gave the usual excuse and went to visit her. We lay on the bed and talked until it was very late—I just couldn't touch her.

She was happy to talk—she says those are the moments when she loves me most. She asked me about my mother and my rich uncle. And I asked her to tell me about her parents, who were living in Oregon with her brother. He hated working in the mechanic shop their father had passed on to him, but it was the only thing he knew how to do. He thought of Lisa as the family intellectual, the first one to go to college and to leave Portland.

I kissed her at last as dawn was breaking, and she took my face in her hands. We held each other tight and made love without saying anything, and she gazed into my eyes the whole time.

I thought about that gaze again when the doctor's report arrived. Lisa needed an operation, right away; she had cancer.

16

"We shouldn't think of sin as representing a greater distance between man and God. Sin's not a distance. It's
a turning of our gaze the wrong way." Father John
said that to me the night before he died. He must
have been worried about the state of my soul. Those
words weren't his, but they had been of great help to
him, even before he decided that he too would lie full
length on the floor in front of an altar. He confided
those words to me that last evening—no telling what
his sins might have been—but then he jerked his head
to one side with a sharp, decisive movement, showing
me that one's gaze must always be turned in the right
direction.

He was the one who'd suggested that I go to Rome
for the Jubilee. "It's an experience that can change
your life," he said. "And it's best that you have it
while you're young." He believed in prayer, Father

John did, and also in repentance and forgiveness. He believed in things we can't understand, even in some that seem stupid and senseless to us. And he believed, like nobody else, in beauty. He would say things like, it's the best way to reach salvation.

I followed his advice without any clear sense of what to expect. The idea of gaining an indulgence had always seemed strange to me: I saw something too human, something mathematical and even commercial in that mechanism of redemption, and he pointed out that it's a weakness to consider God a remote, incomprehensible entity. I wasn't at all convinced, I never am, but I've always been afraid of losing the privilege of my religion. Just as I'm afraid—and have been since I was born—of losing my faith. Afraid of being unable to appreciate its simplicity, and in the same instant to see the abyss of my weakness.

The first thing that came to my mind when I learned of Lisa's illness was the emotion I'd felt several years earlier upon my arrival in Rome. I don't know why I thought of that. It's the Eternal City, I told myself, in such a moment it's what I need. I need beauty that redeems without repentance.

My mother was the first person who ever talked to me about going to Rome. She had traveled there as a child with her own mother, who insisted that she had to see the *Pietà*. When she faced the statue, my grandmother had simply said, "Full of grace," and then she'd become emotional, because no one has ever represented that ideal better than Michelangelo. "In the moment of greatest pain," she'd added, with a smile full of tears.

When my mother told me that story, I felt first fear and then the sense of inadequacy that never leaves me. When I don't know what to say to the person whose confession I'm hearing. When I return home after my nights of sin. And when my words aren't accompanied by feeling but rather hide it. When I can't find the right ones in the face of the reality that annihilates our illusions.

But now that you've put me to the test again, my Lord, I keep thinking about my first day in Rome, because the emotion I felt then was powerful, unforgettable. I was a frail, modern pilgrim, just arrived from the New World, who had perhaps never known what beauty was.

I began to notice it when I saw the first pines, and then the ruins, and then the baroque churches. I even felt a little guilty that morning, crumpled as I was from the long night flight: In the presence of all that enchantment, I hadn't felt anything spiritual, only aesthetic pleasure. And I had too often tried to convince myself that they were the same thing.

I'd been told that there wasn't anything like Rome in October, and while I was entering the city, I'd felt the need to say thanks and then thanks again. Because we're ashes and dust, but we're also capable of creating marvelous things. And because your spirit, Lord, has breathed upon even our unworthiness.

No, it couldn't have been a merely human idea to put an obelisk on an elephant in front of the church of Santa Maria sopra Minerva. And another obelisk in the fountain of the Pantheon, the most mysterious and moving building I'd ever seen. Who could say how much sordidness he'd stained himself with, the artist to whom that flash of inspiration had come? Who could say why God inspired him and only him? And who could say why in that way?

I had entered the city of popes and emperors and artists, knowing that each of them was full of baseness and sordidness. Of violence and cowardice and filth.

I had gone there to ask forgiveness for a sin I would continue to commit, knowing that God would never abandon me; rather it was I who abandoned him, every day.

The eternal beauty of the weary city had suspended all my questions, but faced with that medical report, so clear and pitiless, all I wanted to say was "Why?"

Not Lisa, she didn't ask questions. Those are weaknesses proper to us men.

17

I always run away from problems. I'm a coward like Saint Peter, worse than Saint Peter. So I kept my mind on those October days in Rome and my mother's story about the visit to the *Pietà*. I don't know, maybe thinking about that wasn't much of an escape.

Lisa said she wasn't afraid, because that was the way to defeat every evil.

She was right, I told her, that was the correct attitude, but fear wouldn't have been anything to be ashamed of either; Christ himself was afraid on the Mount of Olives.

And she smiled and said I never stopped preaching. Then she added that nevertheless, she wasn't ready to lose her hair. Our love affair had deprived her of the pleasure of walking arm in arm in public with her gentleman friend, but her vanity was intact. She would buy a copper-colored wig, she said; she'd always dreamed of looking like Maureen O'Hara in *The Quiet Man,* and now her illness would provide her the opportunity.

It was Lisa who took me to see that film one afternoon at MoMA, my heart beating hard with the fear of being recognized and with the joy of being with her. At one point, she even squeezed my fingers, and I got excited while listening to the clatter of the subway as it passed under the museum.

"Abram," she said, and she left it at that, and squeezed my fingers hard, while her favorite actress, up there on the screen, showed that she for her part was afraid of nothing.

That was the night she got pregnant.

I always run away, and I kept on thinking about my trip to Rome and my attempt to purify myself. About Saint Peter's Basilica, crowded with pilgrims, and about the Romans' jaded reaction to them: Over the course of the past two thousand years, they'd seen it all, and nothing could get them worked up, not even such an event. Then I thought about the nuns, walking in groups and silently smiling. Once I saw a most beautiful sister and wondered how many suitors she'd given up. Yes, they really seemed to be in the world but not of the world. I thought about how they lit up when they saw the pope appear in the window of his study, about the simple pride with which they recited the Angelus and then pondered the words of that weary, nasal-voiced pontiff, who within a few years would complain to God about his not having answered a papal prayer.

Shall I ever have that courage, that strength, that passion? Shall I ever have the greatest strength of all, the strength to bow my head?

I was staying with a friend of Father John's, a priest brimming with enthusiasm who had founded a community in Brazil. He wasn't cultured like Andrew, he'd read only religious texts, but he had Andrew's same fervor, and he was following the same path. He too had decided to dedicate himself to the wretched of the earth, and he wanted to know all about the homeless in New York. The poverty-stricken people he ministered to had never even imagined what wealth might be, and one evening we discussed at length which was worse: to lose everything or never to have had anything. He would pray with his eyes closed, I can remember that as if it were yesterday, and he used to say that the only time he felt at home was when he stepped into a church. I hadn't ever thought of that before, and from then on I would ask myself if it was the same for me.

The current pope, he told me, had written an encyclical that had caused quite a stir and even provoked some violent reactions: He'd challenged the world at a moment when doing so seemed impossible, when going against the current meant crucifixion. But isn't that the lot of every authentic Christian, the very essence of our faith?

When I saw him at his Vatican window, he seemed to be such a mild, austere man, a man blessed with doubt: The strength of our ideas has nothing to do with the tone we use.

I knew his *Humanae Vitae* well, I'd read it in the seminary, but I'd never reflected on the fact that it was the last thing the pope would ever write. Maybe the reactions to his encyclical had been traumatic for him; maybe he felt he'd said all he had to say.

He'd written that letter for me too: For whoever embraced Christ, for whoever rejected him. For whoever knew nothing of him, and for whoever considered him history's greatest con man.

The pope had also written his letter for Lisa, who believed that nothing and no one could stand in the way of our love, and who now was fighting for her life. She couldn't be afraid, not someone like her, who had defied God.

18

Before deciding to become a priest, I had made only one other decision with equal conviction: I'd decided to kill myself.

Then I'd realized that life must always prevail, and that only our absurd egos, which cause us to take ourselves seriously, prevent us from seeing the wonder of it. I decided, therefore, to kill myself only insofar as the world was concerned. At least, that's what I thought for a long time, until the day I met the girl in the homeless shelter. After that happened, I told myself I mustn't necessarily be damned for it; Christ himself had taught us that the spirit may be strong but the flesh is weak. Then, during the night, I concluded that it simply wasn't true; there was no great strength in my spirit either.

I understood that then and understand it now when I think about death, which is the thought that has accompanied me since I was born. And also when I think about the salvation to which I've been called to bear witness. And about the beauty whose splendor I'm supposed to magnify.

The call came suddenly, swiftly, faster than an instant, less illusory than time: I felt that the only thing that would make life worth living was to dedicate myself to others, to making them a little happier. At least for a few moments, because if you can be happy once, you can be happy always. And I understood that nothing would offer a better possibility of being happy than spreading the good news, the promise that the last would be first and the meek would inherit the earth.

He promised it to me too; to me, who felt like the most wretched thing on earth, and maybe I was; to me, who will never be meek.

And I felt the joy of silence, of trustfulness, of answering "Yes."

I felt the love of my father, who had given me life in the world. And the love of my mother, who had never wanted anything in return.

And I sensed that peace too could exist in the world, and that I too could understand what grace is.

19

When I'm loving Lisa, I don't feel dead. I don't feel dead at all.

I know I'm betraying my promise, insulting my Savior, putting another nail in his cross, as they told me in catechism, but in that moment, when my heart explodes with pleasure and my muscles tense up, I'm alive. Like her eyes, filled with desire, and her kisses, and her moans. Like my cock when it gets hard.

I didn't feel dead with the girl in the homeless shelter either. No, not even a little.

And not with Dena, who made me come like nobody else: My sins are the life you bestowed on me, my Father who art in heaven.

As for death, I feel its presence at other moments, and every time it comes courting it wants to stay and stay. It caresses me, it smiles at me, it promises me peace.

It tells me to stop deluding myself: Nothing means anything. To grow is to understand, and to embrace death is a sign that one has understood everything, completely. There's no need to be afraid of the void; it's the only thing that exists. And it makes no sense to extend this voyage, which takes us out of nothing and carries us back to nothing.

I feel death when I no longer see you in the eyes of the person before me, my Father who art in heaven, and up there where you are, you can't feel such things. Because during those moments, heaven doesn't exist either.

I feel death when I administer the last rites and promise the sick person true life; the one that's coming to an end is only a passage, I say. But in reality, sometimes I think there won't be anything besides bodily decay and dust. And worms.

The last time I administered the holy oil, I found myself looking at the fingernails of a man who was still young. The sickness in his blood, having brought his body low, was finishing its work. He had little time left, perhaps only a few hours. Nevertheless, when that young man with the extinguished eyes breathed his last, his fingernails would keep on growing, heedless of his death. And so would his hair, which his disease, as indifferent as nature, had thinned out.

Lisa's biopsy report had come on Good Friday, but I resisted making facile connections: There's no day that's not Easter and Christmas, All Saints' Day and All Souls' Day. There's no day that doesn't bring death and resurrection, mud and spirit.

I was in prayer on that day, on the Friday so dark there's not even a mass. Churches without lights frighten me, I admit it; unlit churches make me think about the end of all things. My church is the only home I have, and it, at least, must always be full of light. On that dark day, there's no miracle of the bread that becomes body and the wine that becomes blood. The entire Friday is petrified by the cry that makes my wrists tremble and fills me with anguish and fear: "My God, my God, why have you forsaken me?"

That's what I too feel like crying out, every Good Friday and every day when I'm aware of falling. And I've never been nailed to a cross, nor have I ever saved anyone.

I prayed with my eyes closed, opening them now and then to stare at the crucifix. I'm on the lookout for miracles every waking moment; I was hoping it would speak to me, that wooden statue, hoping it would say something, hoping it would, as always, save me. And I also stared at the stained-glass windows: Without light I'm nothing, I said to myself.

The next day, I finally grasped the meaning of the Saturday before Easter, even though that meaning had been explained to me in the seminary; only pain can help us to comprehend the truth. That day, suspended between a cruel, desperate death and the Resurrection, contains our entire life. The meaning and the greatness of faith are in that day of waiting, of silence, and Lisa showed that she had a lot more faith than I did.

20

"You should be ashamed of yourself, Father."

Those were the only words in the note, but its meaning was clear. Sister Lorraine had brought it in to me with the other mail, and I'd opened it in front of her with a smile on my face. But then the back of my neck felt cold, and I began to perspire.

It was handwritten, and I tried—I don't know why—to figure out whether or not the penmanship was female.

Then I read the rest of the mail with exaggerated attention: the reminder about the Marian prayers for the month of May, the meeting with the parents of the children who were to be confirmed, the cardinal's call to attend the Corpus Christi mass. There was also an invitation to an opening in my uncle Nicola's art gallery; he was convinced that it was his duty to bring me back to the world. He really didn't know me very well. Seeing the invitation gave me the opportunity for another escape, and I started thinking about him and his wife, my aunt Tess. They had no children—there's no saying whether that was a choice or a sorrow—and in any case, we've never spoken about it. I wondered whether they still made love.

Then I shut myself up in my room and obeyed the injunction given me in the note; it was the only right thing to do. And immediately afterward, I felt great relief. I'd been wanting to do that for a long time, I told myself.

Revelation, punishment, repentance, expiation. Purification. Words I studied in the seminary. Words that were to be filled with substance. Faced with them, however, I felt strong, because they didn't apply to me.

Repentance: That was the hardest one, because I wasn't in the least repentant. Even though a part of me had always hoped I'd get caught; I knew I'd never repent on my own.

But then the chill returned, along with the fear: Who'd written that note? Why had they used that particular method? Could I expect more of the same? And what consequences would it cause, to my habit, to my parish, to my faith?

The author of the note had used the word *Father.* Was it sarcasm, contempt, respect?

And how did they know about me? Where had they seen me? At Lisa's? That time at MoMA? Or maybe they were talking about Dena . . . In fact, maybe the writer was Dena herself; this was her way of taking revenge, of getting the last word, of reviving the relationship . . .

I thought for a moment about the bright lipstick she'd worn to church, about her air of defiance, about the way she used to look at me before we had sex. But no, who knew how many men she'd had besides me and that other priest.

And of course I felt shame. It's the feeling I revisit most often, ever since it took the place of joy. But in the present case, the summons to feel ashamed came from without; the note implied that my own sense of guilt was insufficient or nonexistent.

I'd been reminded that I didn't have the strength my mother had, she who could conquer the world through her simplicity. The strength to overcome all logic, knowing that nothing in the world is really logical. It was my mother who had taught me that a crazy person is someone who's lost everything except his reason.

That note reminded me that I also lacked the strength of all the men who had made the same choice as I had, and who unlike me embraced the boredom that besets us every day. My sin was a rebellion against life's mediocrity, which condemned me never to see its inward, poignant wonder.

21

The lines for the confessionals are always long at Easter time. And these days, the people who come to confess prefer a young priest like me to the older fathers. Jorge doesn't say anything, he knows how the world goes, and he offers up even this little humiliation to the Lord.

That Saturday I listened to the usual interminable catalog of betrayals, malfeasances, and thefts. I consoled, welcomed, made the proper references to the Gospel; I'm good at that, and I've always liked to amaze my confreres with my knowledge. Vanity is one of my major sins. I'm not shocked by contemporary attitudes, and I know how to speak today's language, though on a couple of occasions I've gone so far as to raise my voice. That's why people come to me for confession, but they know that behind me I've got a two-thousand-year-old institution, of which I am the symbol, the witness, the embodiment, and the servant.

Human beings are always the same, and what's incumbent upon me to do, what I promised to do when I put on this habit, is to counter, pathetically insufficient as I am, the eternal recurrence of the identical; because it's not me who does the saving, I know that, I've known it since the day I entered the seminary: We're nothing but frail, unwitting instruments.

"You should be ashamed of yourself, Father."

While I continued to hear confessions, those words remained inside of me, resonating, inexorable. They were the very words my own conscience had spoken to me, countless times, and which I had refused to heed.

In my mind's ear, I heard them spoken by a male voice, in a loud tone full of rage and malice. And pain, because I had failed, I too had fallen.

Then I heard a woman's voice say the words; the note-writer must have been a woman, maybe one of those who were confessing their sins at that very moment, and the tone was the same: indignant, resentful, furious at my betrayal. And then broken by grief, shattered, even affectionate.

It was the tone my conscience used when it spoke to me.

I sensed once again the depths of the ruin into which I would drag my habit and my church. I thought about the damage I would cause to my faith, and about my many brother priests, so many, who didn't share my weakness. "Saintliness is mediocre," I said aloud.

Then I thought about the shame on the sisters' faces, on Jorge's face. About the pain I would be giving Father John if he were still alive; it was better that he wasn't.

A woman in her forties was confessing that she and her building's super had become lovers. She insisted on telling me his name: Raul.

She would seize on any excuse to call him, she said, and then she'd get satisfied—this was the term she used. "I can't do without it, Father." It couldn't be her. This woman was speaking to me as if I were a doctor; she wanted to be treated now, and there would be time for absolution later.

"I've become Raul's sex slave, Father." What she didn't add was how much she liked it. She just wanted to regain the freedom to decide, to be the person in charge of her own desire.

I asked her what her name was, because I love details and precision; I like the outlines that stories and lives can be set in, as if that were really possible. "Rosa," she answered, after some hesitation—this seemed to be the only revelation she wasn't ready to make. "Rosa Estrada," she said suddenly. She'd gone that far, might as well confess everything. "I was born in Guatemala, Father, and I'll go back there someday." I told her—who knows why, I've never seen it—that

Guatemala was a beautiful country. Then I talked to her about the importance of repentance and purification, because otherwise I couldn't have administered the sacrament. Her only response was to tell me more stories of her affair. She said that once they'd done it next to her six-month-old baby girl's cradle; the child had kept crying the whole time. Her name was Michelle—Rosa told me that without my asking—and I imagined a little girl identical to her mother, who kept recounting the experience as if it had occurred that very morning.

Maybe it had occurred that very morning.

She added that whenever she did it with her husband, she always thought about Raul, every time. It was during her confession that I raised my voice, but then I tried to control myself, and I told her that I could give her absolution only if she were truly repentant. I was crying, and I must have shocked her.

She retreated into silence. After a long pause she said yes, she did repent, she was really sorry, and she even told me her husband's name: "Nelson, but everybody calls him Sam." Then we both fell silent for a long while, after which I gave her absolution, because it's not for me to refuse anyone an Easter Sunday, a Resurrection day; but we both knew that the emotion she felt would subside as soon as she left the confessional. I watched her walk away and light a candle to the Virgin: She was a shabbily dressed woman with anonymous, ordinary features. I imagined her getting satisfaction with Nelson, whom everyone called Sam, and then with Raul, and I felt disgust.

I was tired that day, tired of listening to so much misery, but the line was long: The harvest is plentiful, and the workers are always few.

And very, very few know how unworthy I am.

I always feel boundless affection for those who come to confess, convinced that they've committed who knows what grave fault, and their infractions turn out to be minuscule. The more laughable the sins are, the more affection I feel. My deepest gratitude goes out to people who are trying in every way possible to attain a state of purity.

The smile on the face of someone leaving my confessional reconciles me with the world: More than anything else, sin is boring.

22

On Easter Sunday I decided to steal a bit more money than usual. It's another day when the offerings are substantial; if it weren't for the Resurrection, our faith would make no sense, as even those who get dressed up and go to church only on Easter realize. I stole three hundred and ten dollars, the last ten inadvertently—they'd been put in an envelope by Rosa Archibald, a lady from Harlem who comes down to us once a year, only on Easter Sunday, and always wears an enormous green hat.

I wanted to do something I hadn't ever done, something Lisa and I would never have been able to do. I arranged to meet her at the Greyhound station without telling her anything else; it was supposed to be a surprise. All she had to do was to be available for a couple of days. In the parish I'd said that I was going to spend Easter Monday—*Pasquetta*, an important

Italian holiday—with my mother. I asked Jorge to pray for her; she wasn't well at all, I said, trying to escape my shame, and besides, I figured a little prayer couldn't hurt.

Even early in the morning, the Port Authority Bus Terminal was full of prostitutes. I remembered that Christ had never denounced them, and that he was, in fact, a friend to them, as he was to thieves. The young men all had long, straggly hair, and even without my priestly habit, I felt like a foreign body, a presence from somewhere out of this world. A pervasive, sweetish odor of maple syrup and beer mingled with the reek of garbage. On the floor under the ticket agent's window, a couple were asleep in each other's arms. They were wearing phosphorescent armlets and necklaces, and next to them lay a guitar; no telling what they were playing while my world was celebrating the Resurrection. The agent looked at them with annoyance, but he didn't have the strength, and probably not even the will, to run them off. A few yards away, next to a doughnut shop, there was a girl whose hair was dyed an electric blond; she was asleep with her head upside down, and beside her extremely pale face was the food she'd vomited up before nodding off. A black man approached to ask me for money, but I'd budgeted everything I had, right down to the last penny, for my trip with Lisa. He had no teeth, and he mumbled something incomprehensible before heading for another passerby.

At that moment, Lisa appeared, wearing the turquoise shawl; it was her way of saying how pleased she was. But she responded to my smile with an inquisitive stare—she hadn't expected to see me without my habit. I had the feeling that the prostitutes understood perfectly well what I was; they have real knowledge of the world. I gazed into Lisa's eyes. She didn't look sick at all.

She seemed to be at her ease even in that place and quickly got on the bus. She couldn't wait to leave. She asked no questions along the way, just rested her head on my shoulder without talking; she trusted me.

We reached Lancaster County, Pennsylvania, three hours later and started to see Amish people riding in their buggies. I myself didn't even know why I'd brought her there.

"They've refused our world," I told her, "but they're called 'the gentle people.'" Lisa smiled. She knew much more about the Amish than I did, beginning with the name of their community's founder, Jakob Ammann. However, she'd never been in those parts before, and she was as happy as a child.

We stayed with a lady who rented a room in her house and had done so ever since she'd lost her husband. She wasn't Amish, but she was fond of those odd people; after all, they indirectly provided her with her living. She explained to us that her daughter had gone off to college in California, and that she, the mother, had discovered what solitude was. She tried to console herself by eating; in the last two years, she'd gained more than thirty pounds.

"She's a mathematician. All her teachers at Stanford have a high regard for her."

She asked if she could join us at dinner and proudly showed us photographs of Karen, her daughter: She was covered with freckles and, like her mother, overweight. Then our hostess offered us some homemade butter, personally prepared by herself. "Tomorrow morning you'll taste my marmalade," she added, and then she wanted to know what my line of work was. I could find no words, but Lisa replied that I was a rabbi; my name worked like a charm.

Later, in bed, we laughed about that together, recalling the way the lady had stared. She seemed to be in awe of my chosen profession. The ambient silence was something we were totally unused to, and from our window we could see all the stars. It had been years since I'd seen them shine. Lisa noticed them too, but we decided to share that enchantment without speaking.

Then, later, at the darkest moment of the night, she started talking to me. She could tell I was awake. "I know I've always been looking, Abram, and I've realized that all we can do in life is to ask questions, without deluding ourselves about finding answers. The same with art, or with religion. We can only keep on looking, keep on looking."

I replied that we wouldn't keep on looking if we

hadn't already found something that gives our existence meaning, but she hugged me tight, tighter than she'd ever done before. "This affair of ours," she said, and then she suddenly stopped talking. Her tone was too severe.

"Our love affair, Abram, and my illness . . ." She stopped again and then resumed, saying the rest all in one breath: "They cause me shame, anger, and fear, but the only words I'll say before I leave will be 'Thank you.'"

She put her hand over my mouth—she didn't want me to say anything. And we stayed that way, holding on to each other, looking at the stars.

Of those two days, I remember our long walks in the country silently inhabited by the gentle people, our visit to a house without electricity and then a store where an Amish girl was selling original products: I bought a quilt with the little money I had left over. On our last afternoon, we went horseback riding. Lisa, who was much better at it than I was, gave me several useful tips. The Amish country reminded her of Oregon, she said, and then she added that the gentle people didn't seem unhappier than the people we saw in New York.

The evening of our return to the city, an electrical storm came up, full of lightning flashes and thunderclaps, and I thought there was no escaping life. The serene expression on Lisa's face as she slept in the bus made me wonder if she was dreaming. The rain beat against the windows, and Manhattan was a colorful, neon-lit mess.

The traffic didn't get any better. At the end of the line, we found a group of hippies singing at the top of their lungs a song about a boxer unjustly sent to prison and denied the possibility of becoming the champion of the world.

23

Don't think that it's only love with me and Lisa; it's also sex, which feeds every sigh, every heartbeat, every thought.

And we play all the time. Lisa says she's never done it like that with anyone else, and I have never desired anything, anything at all, as much as I desire to take her, to possess her, to make love to her.

Whenever we're together, I substitute her for Christ, and while we're doing it, while we're making love, I think that the Son of God was a man, and that he must have felt the same desire. I'm afraid of those thoughts; I feel more fear than shame. And I'm afraid of myself.

Then there are days when I forget her, and it seems absurd to me that I could be having a relationship with a woman. It disappears completely, because I feel that mine is a different life, and my choice of that life is the greatest joy I've ever known, the greatest joy I can ever know. There's nothing like the serenity of grace and the sense of being a child of God, of his love, of playing an infinitesimal but indispensable part in the harmony of the universe. And nothing like seeing my own joy in the eyes of the others whom I've been given the privilege of serving, of helping. Yes, in those moments, Lisa completely disappears, and our relationship seems unnatural, absurd, squalid. Once I even managed to leave her, and for days she seemed insignificant, tiresome, even ugly; I liked nothing about her and quite a bit less about me. And I embraced the rite, as I always do at such times. The rite I saw celebrated in Rome by that pale pope who challenged the world, the rite I see performed every day by so many servants of Christ. I pray there aren't many of them as unworthy as I am. I pray to find the strength, the way. I pray to know how to pray, and sometimes I think that our uniqueness and our strength lie in this very weakness.

Yes, I embrace the rite, or rather I let it embrace me, because only in that ancient liturgy am I able to find the truth. There's no separation between the fragrance of incense and the charity I try to practice in the homeless shelters, between the incessantly repeated litanies and the sandwiches Raj prepares for the homeless.

And it's the truth that frees us—I know the verse by heart, John 8:32. I recite it in almost every homily, and it always moves me. I say, "John 8:32, never forget it, brothers and sisters in Christ: 'And you will know the truth, and the truth will set you free.'"

That was the passage that opened my eyes and changed my life. Ecstatic with joy, I thought that the natural consequence of truth and freedom would be happiness. "Life, liberty, and the pursuit of happiness," as the Declaration of Independence, signed by the dreamers who founded our country, says.

May God never take away our faith, our Father who art in heaven. Or our hope. According to Saint Paul, the greatest virtue of all is charity, and that's the one I believe I still have, still practice. Sometimes, however, I despair of attaining salvation, and that's the gravest sin there is, I know. And I know that I lose life, liberty, and happiness whenever I distance myself from the choice I made, from the choice I wanted. Dearly wanted. I lose life, liberty, and happiness when I distance myself from the only revolution that can be successful, the only one that can make sense.

Noli foras ire, in te ipsum redi, in interiore homine habitat veritas.

Father John had understood everything about me.

Noli foras ire.

Why are the lessons of life, which touch me and make me feel strong enough to overcome the world—why are they always swept away, forgotten, humiliated? And yet the seed must have found fertile ground, otherwise it wouldn't yield fruit.

I answered your call, our Father who art in heaven, but why is my plant choked with so many thorns? Why have you made me so weak, so ready to succumb to the world?

Every time I return to you, I can feel your embrace, the father's embrace of his prodigal son. That embrace is life, I know it, but I'm just as certain that the father knows that each of his children will fall again, and then again. But your embrace is stronger than our weakness, and it's all that keeps me alive.

I always go back to Lisa. Inevitably, inexorably.

And even at that moment, you are at my side.

Even when I see her again and everything else disappears.

It's in her that I place my worldly faith: in the sensuous way she rests her cheek on mine without saying a word. Once she quoted some lines of a poem—I remember it, because it hurt me a lot: "Our infirmities merge, and as though carried away, we remain."

I trust Lisa when we talk after making love, and on the occasions when I don't say anything, she knows every word of my silence. I trust her when I weep; I'm not afraid to do so in front of her. And when I escape into my stories, into my dreams, into my fears.

She knows when I need to let off steam—in bed, I mean. When she gives herself to me and makes me come before she does, before I give her satisfaction. She always smiles at those moments. Tenderly.

But then she has me take her again and she comes

too, she goes mad with pleasure. Her body is small, which makes me seem bigger and stronger and therefore excites me even more. And the little moles on her back excite me too. I always kiss them after I come.

Lisa says she's not a believer. And yet every now and then she goes to Sunday mass, though never at our church. Sometimes I look for her in the congregation, in the hope that she wasn't able to resist.

I always look for her when I speak about the truth that sets us free.

Once I woke up in her bed after a night of love. I noticed that she was praying, but for some reason, she didn't want me to see her doing that.

24

I went with her to her first chemotherapy session. No one frowns on a priest who's accompanying a sick woman. Rather, it's considered an act of charity, one of those gestures that explains the meaning of the habit he's wearing and ennobles it even in the eyes of those who have contempt for it.

While we were in the waiting room, I stared at the other patients' faces, one after the other, and I thought about their individual stories: Everything they'd done, everyone they'd seen, appeared irrelevant in that room. Their existence was being entrusted to the substance that was about to be introduced into their bodies, and which would ravage them in the hope of striking down the disease too. The medicine represented their future, and with it everything that no single body can contain, beginning with desires. The time had not yet come for memories to grow poignant; that would arrive with the certainty of the end, maybe a few days from now.

A young man—thirty at the most—smiled from across the room, his eyes asking me to pray for him. He must have been a Catholic, or maybe just desperate. I smiled back. My mission is to bring hope, I told myself. I'm supposed to know how to talk about many things, including death, which is only a passage to the true life. But the time wasn't right, not just then. I offered a second, weaker smile.

He was sitting next to a very overweight woman. She didn't look sick at all, and she revealed that she'd begun her treatment more than a month ago. She spoke in the complacent tone experts use and sounded as though she were talking about a course of study that had opened new horizons for her. She had on a pair of very conspicuous earrings, and her head was covered by a length of flaming red fabric wrapped like a turban. It was only while contemplating this headdress that I had a sudden realization: All the people in the waiting room were wearing loud clothes. It must have been a way of putting up a fight. The woman smiled at Lisa—she'd make it, there wasn't anything to worry about—and Lisa replied with a pointed gaze; she didn't know how to react to that solidarity. I too looked the expert in the eye, wondering how much time she had left. A droplet of sweat was descending from under her turban.

The most morose patient was a middle-aged gentleman with a sunken face and a yellow complexion. For him, perhaps, the moment of certainty had already arrived. But his eyes contained no plaintiveness—fury, if anything: He was nervously scratching one cheek, unable to accept that just then, of all times, and just there, of all places, he should have to suffer the additional discomfort of an itch.

Lisa was called last and asked me to stay in the waiting room. The doctor was a tall man with an impassive expression, which made me feel better; that's the attitude you need, I thought, when you're confronting evil.

And that's what I continued to think while assessing the traffic outside, the commuters trying hard to get out of Manhattan—from a distance, they all looked the same—and also while we sat in the taxi and I watched a succession of indifferent faces glide past us, rushing and rushing and not knowing exactly why.

I wondered if my sense of fear and emptiness, two feelings I was nevertheless called to combat, was due to my unworthy condition. Or maybe the cause was Lisa's illness. She put her arms around me, held me close, and shut her eyes; she couldn't have cared less about what the cabdriver might think. And in that moment, I didn't care either.

25

When we got back to her place I cut off her hair—it was important to me that I should be the one to do that. And then I put her to bed, looking at her body, which was under attack but still strong. For how long, I wondered.

Without taking off my habit, I remained seated beside her. Up until that moment, she'd never looked so little to me. Her hands were tired, barely able to squeeze mine. Only her eyes appeared larger, deeper. They seemed to have seen everything already.

She asked me to read something to her. I couldn't find anything that inspired me, and so I made up a story. My father, it seems, used to do the same thing.

I told her about the time when I worked on the construction of the world's tallest skyscrapers. Man always defies heaven, I said. I tried to make her feel our excitement as we saw those towers grow, and our enthusiasm when we outstripped the Empire State Building. I told her about the party we organized and threw that night—in secret, because we would all have been arrested. About the girls who came to celebrate and dance, and about the oath we all swore together: We would return to those skyscrapers fifty years later, in 2020, and celebrate there, at the highest point man has ever reached, the magic of that night. We would bring along our children, maybe our grandchildren, and we'd give thanks to life for having given us such a moment. And I told her the names of all the songs we'd sung that night, waiting for the sun to emerge from behind the ocean. Inexorable as life, which always wins.

Lisa smiled, because she liked those songs too: "Scarborough Fair," "April Come She Will," "The Only Living Boy in New York."

I told her about Angelica, a Colombian girl who mangled the English language. Her accent was so sexy that we were all in love with her.

Lisa had never heard me tell such stories—she knew I was making up some of them—but when I talked about that girl, she frowned reproachfully, as if she were jealous. Lisa liked to play.

Then I told her about some of the men who had worked on the towers with me. There was one, a Lakota Indian, who enjoyed walking on steel beams 1,300 feet above the earth. His name was Shappa, which means "Red Thunder," and he had a hooked nose and sunbaked skin. He defied the void unhesitatingly because life is a dream, an illusion, or so he said. And he boasted of being the grandson of the man who had scalped General Custer.

"George Armstrong Custer," he'd repeat, forcefully clenching his fist, as if the scalp were still in his hand: Let no one think he had been subdued by the whites; one day he too would have his revenge.

I don't know why I chose that particular story, and I changed it immediately when Lisa informed me with a smile that she didn't much feel like listening to talk about hair. I smiled too, because you mustn't ever lose your sense of humor, and then I told her about Shappa's friend Luis, a Spaniard, who had lost the love of his life. Or rather, he had lost his life, which was how he put it. That part was true, but at that moment I wanted anything but the truth, and so I told her about the time when Shappa, to win a bet, walked backward on a beam, fearlessly. It was a very windy day, Lisa, and I shut my eyes, I couldn't look at him. At one point he flung out his arms—he looked like an eagle—and kept walking backward, as if it were the most natural thing in the world. One step after another, suspended in midair, 1,300 feet up.

When he put both feet on the rough concrete of the 110th floor, he turned to us defiantly and shouted out his name first in Lakota and then in English, for those of us whose lineage was not so glorious.

"Red Thunder!" he bellowed, and then, louder, "Red Thunder!" And finally, even louder, "Red Thunder!"

His arms were still outspread, and he was looking us in the eyes, us men of good sense and little faith.

That was where I ended the story. I had no idea what significance it might have, but Lisa, with an effort, raised herself from the pillow and gave me a kiss on the lips. Then she slipped under the covers and pulled the Amish quilt I'd bought over her because she was cold.

I felt a desire to pray. Then I felt a need to pray, but I didn't have the courage.

26

When the doctor called me the following morning, at first I couldn't figure out how he had my number; only later did I realize that Lisa must have given it to him. He summoned me to his office, because she'd named me as the person closest to her, the person to call in an emergency.

I hurried to him, letting it be known at the church that there was a sick person who needed my help, an excuse that was, after all, true. The physician received me at once. He wanted to tell me that Lisa's condition was serious, much more serious than I could imagine, but I could tell that wasn't the only reason for his call. No fewer than seventeen of her lymph nodes, he said, had been compromised by the disease, and after her course of chemotherapy was completed, Lisa would have to begin radiation therapy.

He looked at me attentively, interrupting himself with long silences. He didn't seem to suspect the nature of our relationship; in fact, I don't think he did, and his motivation for calling me went beyond the implacability of the medical report.

All of a sudden, he said he had a teenage son, and fatherhood was the most wonderful thing that had ever happened to him. He said he loved his wife, and apart from a couple of little flings, he'd always been faithful to her. "The solidity of our marriage is beyond question, and so is my love for my wife, believe me, Father."

He fell silent again, and I asked him if he wanted me to hear his confession.

Without answering my question, he kept on talking, telling me about his son's refusal to speak to him, and about how it was breaking his heart. He couldn't get over it; he couldn't understand what it was that he'd done wrong. "His name is Patrick. He's named after my father's grandfather, who came here from Ireland to escape famine."

Another long silence. Then he added that Patrick had once told him that he, the father, understood nothing about him and had no idea what his hopes and dreams were. He hated him, the boy said, for what he did, for being always ready to save the lives of others and blind to the persons closest to him.

"And the best part is, the lives of others, I can't even manage to save them, Father."

After another silence, he asked if it was ever really

possible to understand other people, especially the ones you love. He didn't want an answer, however, and said that Patrick was an intelligent boy. And handsome too, he added, and that was the only time emotion made his voice shake a little.

Once Patrick had shouted tearfully at his father, insisting he felt he meant nothing to him, and that was the reason why he hated him. But then, he'd added, he'd been able to overcome that hatred as well, because he'd understood that his father meant nothing to him either. The physician repeated those last few words twice, and I said that was the kind of thing people say in moments of anger; the evil that issues from us doesn't represent what we are.

But the doctor needed to talk and wasn't listening to me.

"I ask myself whether it's worth the trouble to do something noble and useful if we then fail on the most personal level," he said. "And how can we be so weak, how can we fall again and again?" He looked me right in the eyes when he said that, and for a moment I was afraid he knew everything.

At that point, he picked up Lisa's folder. He knew its contents by heart, but he sensed an obligation to show me that he was keeping a close eye on this patient, and that her fate was a matter of personal concern to him.

I told him that if he felt he needed to talk or even to make his confession, he could count on me. He ignored my words, and after glancing at Lisa's folder for the nth time, he said, "Your friend is in serious condition—it's best that you know that. Extremely serious. She trusts you, and you'll be able to do more for her with your presence and your affection than you can possibly imagine."

He put the folder on his desk and concluded, "I'm not a believer, Father, but should you consider praying for her . . . it surely wouldn't do her any harm."

27

I returned to the parish with a head full of thoughts and found an ambulance parked in front of the church door. Before I had time to figure out what was happening, I saw two emergency medical technicians approaching, carrying Father Harrigan on a stretcher; he'd had a heart attack. I instinctively went to them and discovered that he was as white as chalk, with staring eyes and traces of froth around his mouth. Sister Lorraine walked beside the stretcher, squeezing the old priest's hand, and Jorge was following her. Father Lowry had stayed behind—he didn't want to be in the way—but Marlon was there with the others, looking devastated; he must never have been grazed by death before.

Sister Beatrice told me that Father Harrigan had suddenly collapsed in the sacristy, and they'd all been convinced that he was dead, but the ambulance men said they'd reached him in time, cases like his were routine occurrences.

It was a glorious day, one of those days that spring bestows on New York every year. The flower beds were filled with orange tulips; the multicolored, invincible traffic throbbed on. In that atmosphere of joy and energy, it seemed unnatural that we should be there, hoping for our brother's recovery.

As the ambulance disappeared, heading east, we followed it with our eyes. The curious onlookers who had gathered in front of the church were milling around in some confusion, as if they'd thought such things couldn't happen to people like us, people in religious orders. Father Harrigan's sister arrived at that moment and seemed irritated to find that he'd left without her. She limited herself to asking what hospital he was being taken to, and then she disappeared again, together with her husband, a little old man with gentle eyes who must have been bossed around every day of his married life.

I hurried back inside. I wanted to talk to Lisa, I needed to talk to her, and as I was moving in the direction of the room with the only telephone in the church building, Sister Lorraine told me that a lady had called and asked for me twice.

I blanched; Lisa must be feeling really bad to commit such a folly. And I mumbled something to justify the calls: The lady was a tiresome parishioner, the sort of person who identified her problems with the problems of the universe.

I decided to go to my own room; Father Olympian was using the phone, and I needed to calm down. I took up the Bible, always the best place to start. I read a few verses of my favorite Psalm:

The Lord is my shepherd; there is nothing I lack.

No, I shall not, I lack nothing, only a spoiled child and a blasphemer can think otherwise. I read those words again, aloud, and then I went on:

Even though I walk through the
valley of the shadow of death,
I will fear no evil;
for you are with me.

I even smiled a little before going on:

Indeed goodness and mercy will pursue me
all the days of my life.

The poetic beauty of the Psalms had beguiled me ever since I was a little boy, but studying them in the seminary made me realize that their beauty is inseparable from their other attributes and exalts their glory.

Merciful and gracious is the Lord,
slow to anger, abounding in mercy.
He will not always accuse,
and nurses no lasting anger;
He has not dealt with us as our sins merit,
nor requited us as our wrongs deserve.

I've always been moved by that passage, as by the one that reminds me who I am and what I'm living through:

Since my heart was embittered
and my soul deeply wounded,
I was stupid and could not understand;
I was like a brute beast in your presence.

I always wonder what there is in me that's bestial, and whether it's true that

Though my flesh and my heart fail,
God is the rock of my heart, my portion forever.

I missed Lisa in that moment and anxiety nearly overcame me, but the telephone was still in use.

When Sister Lorraine came and told me that the lady was on the line again, I felt my heart in my throat. I went back to the telephone room, feigning calm, even boredom; then I carefully closed the door behind me and picked up the receiver.

"Lisa, how are you? It's crazy for you to call me, but I'm so glad to hear your voice."

She said nothing, and I added, "I miss you so much."

After a moment of livid silence, I heard the voice on the other end of the line say, "Shame on you, Father. I'm not your Lisa."

A freezing blast ran up my back and then reached my temples.

"You are a disgrace to the habit you wear, to the promise you made to Christ, and to the sacraments you administer every day. You're an unworthy person, Father."

So this was who had written that note to me: a rather elderly woman with a tense voice. She was completely right, and I didn't have the strength to contest anything she said.

"I've given this a lot of thought, and I've decided to report you to the bishop. If I told your story to the newspapers, I'd end up harming a great many other priests, honorable priests who don't deserve to be tainted with your unworthiness."

I instinctively clutched my rosary and then looked around for the Psalm I'd been reading, but I'd left my Bible in my room.

"Maybe one day you'll repent for what you've done, and maybe Almighty God will forgive you. As for me, I can't; I can't feel anything for you but anger and contempt."

Then she said something incomprehensible and

violently hung up. And I remained in the telephone room for a long time, asking the Lord for the strength to accept the humiliations and the punishments I'd earned.

I stared and stared at the crucifix—there's not a room in the church building that doesn't have one. I looked our Savior in the face, trying to understand how he was looking at me in that moment.

It was the same image I saw every day; the crown of thorns was identical too, as were the wound in his side and the nails that pierced his feet and his hands.

28

When I heeded the call of faith—the name for it in the seminary—I understood I would need a model to follow. That too had been taught me by my teachers in those ardent days, and it was a subject that Father John and I spoke about all the time. "Even the greatest men are small, Abram, but we have to learn from them all, and there are some who have given the mystery of existence its proper form." Father John spoke in a dry voice, and he always reminded me that mine was a hard name to live up to, perhaps even too hard. Then he added that the angels manage to fly because they don't take themselves too seriously: He'd read that in some book and remembered it, even though—unlike me—he preferred to forget quotations. He believed in angels, he felt their protection and guidance. And he believed in devils, men and women like us, overcome by their own pride.

If I consider carefully, it was the models I chose who made me hear the call, who told me that kindness wasn't impossible, and maybe holiness wasn't either. When I talked about such things, my friends thought I was nuts; the very idea of faith seemed absurd, and talking about saints was ridiculous.

But men who had abandoned everything for an idea, or rather for a promise, fascinated me, they made me feel alive. And when I thought about the choices they'd made, what looked ridiculous to me was my friends' bewilderment. If I learned to combat the sin of pride, I owe that to Father John, but we both knew I would never be able to defeat it.

"With that name you got, you should be a rabbi," Emilio had said. He was a Mexican worker with bloodshot eyes who was always accompanied by a black man from Alabama. Unlike Andrew, Emilio had no idea what a shtetl was, and there was no malice in his words. I'd replied that my mother had started bringing me to church when I was a baby, and that I had just kept on going to church, even by myself: I liked Latin, the solemn language that unified the faithful in every part of the world. *"Ite, missa est."* How I loved that closing formula. No other language, no dialect could so powerfully render that fearless reassurance, the promise that revolutionizes the world.

In addition, I liked the slow, inexorable liturgy, the prayers, the smell of incense and candles. The faces of the images, the statues and paintings: faces of those who suffered in order to bear witness to the good news. And I was devastated by the idea of a God who had sent his own son to be crucified for us. Who had humbled himself so far as to be tormented in the flesh.

The Mexican called himself a Catholic, but I remember his look of consternation and confusion when I said that I also liked the carnality of the Church of Rome, so different, in that respect, from every other religion. "Don't you find that really touching, Emilio? A God with a throbbing pulse, a God who feels pain and delight like any man, and we worship him with our miseries and our fallacious luxuries." Emilio didn't know the word *fallacious,* but he grasped the sense, and he didn't say anything when I added that the church's acceptance of the flesh was the reason why I found the Protestants' choice cold, distant, and not very human. One day I explained to him that their churches lacked earthly joy, they lacked the body, and this lack ended by killing the soul too. Emilio nodded, half smiling at my declaration, but his Alabama friend answered me harshly: There was nothing like a Baptist service, and I didn't know what I was talking about. Jesse—that was his name—was a giant over six and a half feet tall. Once he'd told me that his grandfather had been born a slave, and that no white person could ever understand the psychology of someone who descended from men and women put in chains for the color of their skin.

Jesse never raised his voice, having learned from his

ancestors how useless that was. On the day in question, he stared into Emilio's bloodshot eyes and began to sing "Amazing Grace," as if he wanted to save him from the assertions I'd just made.

He sang the entire hymn, proudly smiling the whole time, then when he'd finished, he added that no Catholic priest would ever have the heart and the musicality of a Protestant pastor.

How I miss those discussions; how I wish that the saints before whom I have bowed my head would help me find the way again.

Joan of Arc, where are you? I took you as my first model: Although you were an illiterate peasant girl, you succeeded in turning disheartened men into warriors and victors. And you faced the flames, while my courage vanishes at every tiny gust of wind.

Then for a brief period it was you, Saint Francis, because you really did abandon the world, facing up to both your father and the pope along the way. I'll never have your purity, I know that; neither animals nor saints will speak to me.

Saint Thomas More, you are beside me in my happiest moments: How admirable I find your courage to say no to your king, a vulgar and brilliant lecher who was also your friend. How inspired I am by the strength with which you faced the scaffold rather than deny your faith, and how I love your irony. Yes, Father John is right, holiness must be light, not heavy; we're too sacred to take ourselves seriously.

But then, with the passage of time, I realized that no saints fascinated me so much as the warriors, maybe because I fight the biggest war inside myself: Ignatius, first of all, and Paul, the persecutor of Christians who became the pillar, sap, and inspiration of the church itself.

They don't seem to have had much of a sense of humor; once again, I understood that the truth can be in anything as well as in its opposite.

And I understood that I have no real model apart from Peter, in his weakness and in his denial of him who had given him the keys to his church.

29

I'm afraid of stillness—I've known that since I was a child. Afraid of silence, of peace.

Of contemplation, of meditation, of everything that should form the essence of my chosen way of life. I'm afraid of life itself, when it pauses to be loved, enjoyed, known.

I'm afraid of the void, of "dead time," which I know is never dead. I'm afraid of prayers without result, and I'm afraid of the faith, yes, of the faith, as I am of any promise that has no certainties.

I decided to be a simple parish priest when I discovered that the Jesuits, before they're ordained, remain silent for an entire month. An entire month. And that for them, obedience is *perinde ac cadaver*. They obey with spiritual delight and perseverance (as they explained to me), but always and without exception: even when their superiors are obtuse, or hypocritical, or idiotic. And even when they're in the wrong, because our Lord's will is greater than our mediocrity, and because divine Providence exists and straightens the paths our wretchedness has made crooked.

I quarreled with God on that occasion too—it's one of my ways of loving him—and then I chose to give up the idea of becoming a soldier in the Society of Jesus; this was, I told myself, an act of humility. And yet I wanted Saint Ignatius to feel that he was my model and that at least I had tried. Íñigo López de Loyola exhilarated me, but I was afraid of him too: Of his solemn name, of his austerity, of his strictness, of the atrocious pain his shattered leg caused him. Of his continuous, implacable questions about the reason for our existence. And of his answers, which postulated a call to change, to transform, to be renewed. All of them were resolutions that I espoused enthusiastically, and which I watched myself fail to keep every day.

The evening after I got the telephone call, I made love to Lisa tenderly, and then furiously. I kissed her nacreous breast, where the disease had done its evil work, and then her neck, her sides. Her crotch.

I wanted to make her feel that I loved her like my life, like my soul; the malady spreading inside her body would defeat us in that way too.

I didn't tell Lisa anything about what had happened: The woman's threat had to remain my problem alone. Later, deep in the night, when she was curled up against my body, I decided to tell her that I'd had other girls. She was shocked. "Before you," I swore to her, and she squeezed my fingers without saying a word; she loved my frailty.

Then I made love to her again, because she was going to grow weaker and weaker with every passing day, and soon we wouldn't be able to do it anymore. I felt ashamed of this thought, but it was what Lisa was thinking too, and she responded to me with the same tenderness, the same fury. We climaxed and wept.

30

I requested an appointment with the bishop the next morning, and he immediately fixed a time for me; maybe the anonymous lady had already informed him. Before going to our meeting, I said mass, trying to look Sister Lorraine and Sister Beatrice in the eye, but their purity is never contaminated by predictable responses. Jorge asked us to pray for our brother in the hospital, and I did so wholeheartedly, but then, in the darkness of my soul, I thought that the sickest person of all was me, and that my greatest sin was my failure to put myself in a position where I could be helped. At the end of the service, I stayed in the chapel alone and offered up to the Lord the humiliation I was about to undergo, praying that it might be in exchange for Lisa's recovery. She found herself in this affair because I had wanted it so, and thus I was the one who ought to be punished.

While on my way to see the bishop, I thought about the way we had looked at each other, Lisa and I, on the day when we realized what was about to happen: There would be no going back. Our eyes said it; our excited breathing required it.

A few weeks before that day, she had started coming to the church as a volunteer to assist the homeless. She called them "the last," with the smile of one who means "the first."

She showed up at seven sharp every morning and helped Raj prepare the sandwiches. She was meticulous and fast, and occasionally she brought some food from home. You have to be generous with the mayonnaise, she told our Indian friend, and when his back was turned, she piled on the cheese and the salami slices too.

One morning I saw that the nape of her neck was covered with little beads of sweat. I tried to turn my eyes elsewhere, but then I watched her movements as she put up her hair. Before she left, she stopped to say goodbye. We were about to have breakfast, and Sister Lorraine invited her to sit down with us; she can't ever have imagined, good Sister Lorraine, the responsibility she bears in all this.

Lisa told us she was studying art history, and she wasn't sure she believed in God. But if an artist was capable of painting the *Primavera,* there must be something much greater that had inspired such harmony, such perfection. I'd never heard the names she mentioned: Botticelli, Pontormo, Bronzino, Lotto. She said that her greatest desire was to see the Scrovegni Chapel in Padua, and she explained to us that the marvelous decorations had been commissioned by Reginaldo, the head of the Scrovegni family, as expiation for the sin of usury. And maybe also as a way of keeping the church happy, but in any case, she concluded with a smile, a disreputable situation had given birth to grace and beauty.

That morning, I remember, I accompanied her to the door and stood there watching her as she walked away, while the homeless people were smiling at me in gratitude for their mayonnaise-lathered sandwiches. Marlon said that he wanted to study those artists—you should never shut yourself off from the world, he said. Jorge seemed a bit miffed because there had been no mention of any Spanish artist, but Sister Lorraine was smiling; she knew that young woman admired her.

Then I remember the telephone call I made to Lisa right after the evening mass, and how I thanked her for what she'd said about art, Providence, and life: "I'd like to talk to you some more—even tomorrow, if possible."

As I stepped into the bishop's office, I tried to forget all the rest, the whole maddening series of events of the past few weeks: In the beginnings of everything, there's still purity.

I saw a portrait of the pope with the nasal voice, and another picture taken when he'd visited New York: In the photo, the pontiff was accompanied by the bishop, who received me with the look of one who'd learned too long ago that nothing in this world can surprise us.

There was only one memory I couldn't manage to expunge from my mind: the way Lisa clutched the sheets when we came together.

31

The bishop was an elderly man who would never be made a cardinal. Maybe that wasn't something he really aspired to, but it was what everyone in the city said about him.

He limped slightly, the result of a war wound, and once he told me it was the only thing he had in common with Saint Ignatius. He had a twin sister who was afflicted by severe mental disorders; her condition was what caused him the greatest distress in life, and the subject made it difficult for him to maintain the contagious serenity that had otherwise brought him widespread popularity, even among nonbelievers.

Don't think, however, that he wasn't an astute man. He had passionately and devotedly followed the work of the Second Vatican Council, fully aware of our church's inescapable challenges, and throughout he'd remained close to Cardinal Spellman, whom he'd accompanied in all of the cardinal's travels. When I met the bishop for the first time, he spoke to me about his fascination for the Latin language: The council's liturgical changes were what he'd found least convincing about that historic turning point.

He received me with unaffected, unfussy warmth, typical of certain elderly priests, and invited me to take a seat in an armchair while a nun served us tea and cookies; they seemed much better than the ones we ate in the parish. On his desk was a photograph of him and his sister. Their physical resemblance was striking, but the woman had a frozen smile.

The bishop sipped his tea and remained silent; he didn't know the reason for my visit. The lady hadn't called him, at least not yet.

I wasn't sure how to conduct myself. I was relieved by the fact that he didn't know anything, and I realized that I wasn't up to making a full confession, I wasn't ready, maybe I never would be.

"I heard about Father Harrigan," he said suddenly. "How is he doing?"

"He's in serious condition, but they say he's going to make it."

He looked me straight in the eye; for a person of faith, life and death take on different values. Then he smiled. "What did you want to talk to me about?"

No, I wasn't ready. Much better to let it slide, to postpone it, until the time came and the case exploded.

Assuming that it was destined to explode: Maybe that lady would never say anything.

I didn't answer for a few seconds, and then I said something that surprised even me: "I wanted you to hear my confession, Your Excellency."

"And you came here especially for that? There are so many fine priests, in your parish and elsewhere . . ."

"I feel as though I can trust you."

"You must trust anyone who wears this habit, Father Abram, even the frailest and most mediocre of us: We're all sinners, but God trusts us. Surely I don't have to teach you that."

He got up from his desk, took a few steps, and sat down beside me. Then he made the sign of the cross and waited for my confession: He'd invoked the power that God had conferred on him, and I felt its entire weight.

"Father . . . Excuse me, I mean Your Excellency . . ."

He smiled, and so did I. Then I started to talk as I had never done before.

"I don't believe in God anymore."

After a silence, I continued, with my eyes closed: "I believe in nothing. Nothing but the void. And in a few moments of occasional pleasure, which dissolve, like everything else, into nothing."

I tried to imagine nothingness and saw myself naked in bed.

Then I saw a chasm, dark and bottomless, that made me sweat.

"I believe in the flesh and in death, Excellency."

I found the strength to open my eyes again before concluding: "I'm afraid of myself."

Basically, I wasn't lying, I thought, but I didn't know how to go on; I didn't have the courage.

"It's not true that you don't believe, Father, otherwise, you wouldn't be here. I think you still want to love our Lord, in whom you say you don't believe. I think you want to beg his forgiveness."

He spoke those words with a smile—I hadn't told him anything he hadn't heard before—and then he said, "But there's an important question I must ask you, a question you must ask yourself: Are you ready to beg his forgiveness?"

Maybe he'd understood everything. Avoiding his eyes, I found myself looking at the photograph of him with his sister, and at her sickly smile.

I didn't say anything; I didn't have the strength. And I was hoping that he'd interpret my silence as assent. One of my greatest sins is underestimating people.

He went on: "There are saints who lost their faith for many years—did you know that? And men and women of faith who sinned throughout their lives but kept doing good the whole time, and they have remained models. The important thing, Father Abram, is never to close the door to the Lord but to continue to speak to him, without fear and without pride."

I don't remember what else he said to me, because I burst into tears.

I went away without saying anything about Lisa, and I received an invalid absolution. At least I think it wasn't valid, because God goes down roads we don't know, and maybe the bishop knew them a little better than I did. He put a hand on my forehead and used all the emphases of the Latin formula: *"Ego te absolvo a peccatis tuis in nomine Patris, et Filii, et Spiritus Sancti. Amen."*

Then, before I left, he embraced me hard, telling me not to fall into the blasphemy of pessimism—that was how he defined it.

And he thanked me for having come to see him.

New York was glorious that morning. As I stepped out onto the street, I thanked the Lord in whom I'd said I no longer believed, and I felt free to sin again.

32

I'd wanted to pay for the abortion myself, but I never told her that the money I had was stolen. I'd paid in cash, without looking the doctor's assistant—a black lady with other things to think about—in the eye.

Now Lisa's insurance is paying her medical expenses; otherwise, we wouldn't have any idea what to do. Nevertheless, I know her well, and I know she would never accept anything from me. "One has to earn death for herself," she told me a few evenings ago.

But she lets me have my way when it comes to our Sunday dinners; they've become a ritual she likes a lot. These days we don't go out anymore—she doesn't feel up to it—and so we have food delivered, usually Chinese, which she can't resist. I can. It's a cuisine I've never appreciated, and now, as far as I'm concerned, that sweet-and-sour stuff has become the food of disease.

We eat in bed and watch reruns of *The Honey-mooners* on television. Lisa laughs like a little girl and lets herself be transported to that black-and-white world where everything always ends well. Then she hugs me and looks out the window at the lights of New York. "It's a fearless city," she told me one night, "because it has welcomed people who were alone."

I've always wondered if there's any living person who isn't, deep down inside, alone, starting with Lisa herself. But she's not afraid, and in that too she's different from me: For her, every problem represents a starting point, not a conclusion to worry yourself to death about. I've seen solitude in the largest, closest families. I've seen it in schools and working groups. I've seen it in protest marches, with everyone shouting together for a cause, and also in churches, in the eyes of the faithful who come to look for hope. I've seen it among people both rich and homeless, among artists and office workers, and I see it every morning when I look in the mirror and ask Almighty God not to abandon me, my God, I implore you not to abandon me, because you alone have saved me and continue to save me.

And maybe Lisa doesn't represent a moment of sin but of salvation: There are things we can't understand, and yet you've given us the freedom to choose, to determine who we are. And I made a promise, I prostrated myself before you, my Father.

I don't touch her anymore, I can't, and I don't know

if she'd want me to anyway. And I don't know how much she misses our lovemaking. Her face is swollen, and her eyes have become small. But the light hasn't left them, and her voice is as bright as ever, rejecting pain and fatigue. Every time I show up, she puts on her Maureen O'Hara wig; she doesn't like to be seen bald. And she doesn't want me to notice what an effort it costs her to do the most normal things, like getting out of bed and going to the bathroom. She tries to move in a natural way, but she suffers terribly: The doctor explained to me that the disease was grinding her bones into talcum powder, to use his expression.

One Sunday I got a substitute to say the evening mass and went to Lisa's early. Let them think what they want, back there in the church. She was vomiting when I came in, and she looked at me angrily; that moment of pain and revulsion was one of her privileges.

She didn't say anything; she didn't have the strength. She got back in bed and started reading a book of Emily Dickinson's poems. She leaned her head on my shoulder, and before long she was asleep.

That I did always love,
I bring thee proof:
That till I loved
I did not love enough.

That I shall love alway,
I offer thee
That love is life,
And life hath immortality.

This, dost thou doubt, sweet?
Then have I
Nothing to show
But Calvary.

She was sure I'd read it too, I know her well.

33

It was ten o'clock that evening when I heard a knock at the door. I woke up with a start; nobody ever comes to Lisa's place. She was sleeping soundly, wrapped up in the covers—she's always cold—and I didn't want to wake her.

I went to the door without turning on a light, peered through the peephole, and saw a very thickset young man who looked both tired and familiar. Sensing my presence on the other side of the door, he said, "Lisa, it's Arthur, open up."

I opened the door noiselessly, and the young man looked at me first with surprise and then with bewilderment.

He had a backpack and muscular arms. He asked, "Is this Lisa's apartment?"

I nodded and informed him that she was asleep in the bedroom. We shouldn't make any noise, I said.

The young man gazed into my eyes incredulously and then, all of a sudden, said, "So it's true . . ."

Priests aren't hard to spot, I thought, and I closed my eyes; I couldn't withstand that searching gaze. He repeated "It's true . . ." with dismay, with sorrow, and with mounting anger, which was visible in the way his graceless body shook.

"What are you doing here?" he asked through clenched teeth, trying not to shout. But then he punched the door, which echoed around the landing.

He grabbed me by the shirt and yanked me toward him. "What are you doing here?"

He repeated the question with fury, with desperation, and then he threw me violently against the wall and raised a fist to strike me. But he struck the door again instead; maybe I wasn't even worthy of being punished.

"What are you doing in Lisa's life? Aren't you ashamed?"

I didn't say anything. I couldn't figure out who he was, but I'd been expecting this moment for a long time.

"Guys like you don't even know what shame is."

He slammed me against the wall again and then hit me hard on the nose, splitting it open.

I brought a hand to my face, which was covered with blood. He hit me again, this time landing a ferocious punch on my jaw and knocking me flat.

"You make me sick, holy man!"

His third blow was a kick in the ribs, and then he started yelling, louder and louder:

"Motherfucker!

"Motherfucker!!

"MOTHERFUCKER!!!"

He wanted everyone in the building to hear. And I didn't try to stop him because I deserved no better.

Neighbors started to come out into the corridor.

Only then did I realize that Lisa had come out too. She'd grabbed the fellow by his shoulders, and she was trying to hold him back.

"Stop, Arthur! For me! Stop it!"

The young man turned, looked at Lisa, and froze. Meanwhile, I touched my ribs and then my nose; it was swollen and felt broken.

Arthur threw his arms around Lisa and burst into tears. And although she could hardly stand up, she consoled him. While he buried his head in her bosom, sobbing all the while, Lisa shot me a look full of tenderness, and I decided to leave; I was ashamed for her too.

As soon as she realized what I was doing, Lisa came over to me and said, "Wait, where are you going? You can't leave like this."

She didn't have her wig on—I hadn't noticed that before.

The youth stayed in his corner and looked at me, breathing hard. A very elderly man, a neighbor who had heard the shouting, approached us, followed by a lady in a dressing gown. They seemed more curious than concerned.

Lisa told them there was nothing to worry about, they could go back inside, and then she took my arm to help me walk. I whispered—softly, I didn't want anyone else to hear—that it would be better for me to go, and that I felt bad for having put her in that situation. I'd come and see her tomorrow, I said.

How swollen she was that evening. And pale, as I saw, but only then.

"You have to forgive him," she said. "He's always been impulsive . . . I beg your pardon in his name."

I didn't say anything. I hoped the pain would make me feel better. But I still couldn't understand.

"He must be really tired, along with everything else. He just arrived by bus from Oregon . . . I didn't know he was coming, he wanted to surprise me."

With difficulty, I set out for the elevator, while behind me the neighbors' doors closed, one after the other. The old man gave me a dirty look, even though I was the one who'd been beaten up. I turned around one last time, and then I saw how much the young man looked like Lisa. I thought he must be her brother.

34

I managed to go back to the church and my room without attracting notice—it was late. And before going to bed, I personally washed the bloodstains off my habit.

Sleep never comes when it should. And that night, not even weeping helped: I felt only the anguish of one who doesn't know how to oppose the evil he causes. And who sees that the mud we're made from soils the spirit too.

Sister Beatrice and Sister Lorraine rushed to help me when they saw me the next morning. I claimed I'd been mugged on the street, and they preferred not to say anything.

Jorge, on the other hand, was worried by what had happened. He asked me if I wanted to file a complaint.

"No, indeed not," I said. "It was just two boys, two dopeheads." That detail added to the sum of my shame.

Jorge said he had good news: Father Harrigan was getting better, and they were going to release him from the hospital in the course of the following week. The tough hearts of the Irish, he added, and then started talking about parish-related matters that needed to be dealt with: We had to make an appeal to our parishioners for the restoration of the church organ; we had to find a way to fund the repair of the electrical system; we had to discuss the preparations for Advent and Christmas; and there was a lady who wanted to donate a genuine Neapolitan *presepe,* a Nativity scene, but setting it up would involve significant expense.

I went to the hospital in layman's clothes, not my priest's habit. I felt sure that any remark the sight of a battered priest might elicit would strike me as the wrong thing to say. At least as long as said priest was me.

The physician on duty told me that my nasal septum was broken, and that from then on I would have a boxer's profile. He seemed amused; maybe he too had figured out who I was. His manners were brusque—he routinely dealt with cases a lot more serious than mine—but he had an easygoing way of displaying his political preferences. A campaign button left over from the last election was pinned to his white coat: *Gimme Jimmy.*

"Your jaw, on the other hand, shows no sign of fracture," he said, and then he added, smiling, "Father." Who did I think I was fooling, I asked myself, while the doctor was explaining that the bruise on my face would gradually disappear.

He told me goodbye and hurried off to examine a black girl who'd been stabbed in the neck and was looking around with wide-open eyes: She couldn't believe that such a thing had happened to her, of all people.

I waited all day to call Lisa. Before I did, I asked Jorge to let me take his place on confession duty; I always do that when I'm feeling bad.

The misery of the world never changes, but that afternoon Rosa Estrada came to see me. She wanted to tell me she'd managed to break off her relationship with Raul. She'd done it for her little girl, she said, but she felt as though she'd had the wind knocked out of her, because her affair with Raul had been about more than sex. However, she knew she'd made the right choice, and now she only needed to find the strength to love her Sam, and she wanted me to pray for her: Maybe the reality is that she'd never loved him.

She added that my severity had been what convinced her; she'd never known a priest who talked to her so forcefully, and for that she thanked God.

Now she was asking me to pray that she wouldn't fall back into sin, because she thought about Raul every day, every hour, every second, and she remembered all the things they'd done, things she was dying to do right then, at that very moment.

She stopped talking for a moment and then apolo-

gized: You don't talk that way to someone who represents Jesus on earth.

I thought back to her words later, when I called
Lisa on the telephone. She immediately asked me how
I was; she'd been worrying about me.

"No, I'd rather hear about how you are," I replied,
but she limited herself to telling me that we'd talk on
the weekend, after Arthur's departure.

Before hanging up, she said softly—her brother
must have been there—"I miss you." She'd never told
me that before.

35

When I got back to the church from the hospital, I found my mother in the little office where the mail gets sorted and candles are sold. It's a tiny, window-less room, also used for hearing confessions during the hours when the church is closed, and for storing the parish bulletins left behind at the end of mass, which nobody has the nerve to throw away. There are some that go back to the 1960s.

She'd been waiting for more than an hour, and when I came in she was looking at a postcard celebrating the pope's address to the United Nations. She knew noth-ing about what had happened to me. I cut her ques-tions short by saying that I'd had a little accident, but I was getting better already; I wasn't cheeky enough to hand her the story about the young, dope-addled mug-gers. In any case, she didn't seem particularly troubled by the way I looked. She said, "I had an urge to see you in your uniform."

She smiled. We see each other so rarely. I hugged her tight, and she told me that everyone had been very nice to her, and at least one of the nuns was definitely happy that she'd come to visit me.

She was wearing a dowdy dress that wrapped up her sexagenarian's body like a bundle. She has never taken care of herself, but she stays fit somehow. She must have been very attractive at twenty years old, I thought, and suddenly I felt embarrassed, while she kept smiling at me in her defenseless, invincible way.

She told me she thanked the Lord, because having a son with a vocation is a blessing, and the world needs hard choices and role models. But she knew how difficult it was, and that morning she'd awakened with the idea of figuring out which parent I resembled more, her or my father. "Neither of us ever became anything great," she added, "and sometimes that's a blessing too." She smiled again, but with a hint of melancholy I'd never noticed in her before.

She came to visit me no more than once a year, and she didn't talk much, but that was her way of telling me that she loved me and that she knew all my frailties.

That day she talked even less than usual and kept gazing into my eyes, as if she wanted to make me understand that nothing escapes a mother. Or maybe that was just what I feared or, who knows, what I wanted.

She decided to leave all of a sudden, as she always did; she'd done the thing that was dear to her heart. She gazed at me one last time, peering deep into my soul, and said, "That's a beautiful uniform you're wearing."

As soon as she left, Jorge asked me to meet him in his office. He never does that; he detests formalities and displays of authority. And then there's his office, which is anything but intimidating: a room with a Formica-topped desk, some books, a crucifix, and a faded photograph of the pope.

He knows everything, I thought, the lady has surely called him. He received me with what seemed like a melancholy air, but maybe not; maybe the wine he'd drunk just made him look blurry.

"Abram," he said. He wanted to stress the responsibility associated with my name. Then he fell silent, looking serious, before saying again: "Abram . . ." It sounded almost like a call for help.

"The sisters have discovered that money is missing from the collection offerings every Sunday."

He stared at me, shaking his head bitterly, and then added, "There's not much money involved, but it's a serious matter."

I nodded, avoiding his eyes, and he went on, reluctantly.

"I spoke to Raj this morning and asked him not to

come anymore. I thanked him for the work he's done for the homeless. The Lord will surely reward him for that, but for the rest, a relationship of trust has been broken, and it's better to cut it off at once, better for him and better for us. It was very hard for me, he's a fragile boy, he needs so much affection."

I couldn't believe my ears. "But how can you be so sure it was him?"

"It's Raj who collects and counts the money."

I felt the necessity of reacting, of protesting, of telling the truth, but I couldn't do it, once again I wasn't ready, and the thought of what I'd become nauseated me. I kept quiet, letting the blame and the disgrace fall on the Indian boy who joked around with me while he made sandwiches for the homeless.

I was breathing hard, but Jorge had already archived the matter; it wasn't the only reason why he'd summoned me.

"I have to go away for a few weeks—health reasons—and I want you to run the parish. You're the only one who can. I've already notified the other priests, and the sisters are in agreement as well."

Then he listed the problems that had to be managed and asked me to supervise the offerings personally until he returned. He was going to a detox center, that was clear, and he was aware that I understood him. "We're all frail, Abram," he said, "and we all need prayers."

36

I felt a great need to go out, which I did immediately after dinner, when the priests and nuns gathered in front of the little black-and-white television set. That evening's broadcasts included a quiz show that greatly amused the two sisters; they were very good at anticipating the contestants' responses.

"I need some fresh air," I said, and nobody asked me to justify myself. The bruise on my face had turned dark, and my nose was swollen; I had the impression that it creaked with every breath I took. The flesh is always weak, I thought.

Attracted by the brightness in the distance, I walked on Broadway toward Forty-Second Street. Rain had fallen on Manhattan all day long, and now the asphalt reflected the neon lights of the theaters, the second-run movie houses, and the sex shops.

Down at the southern end of the island, I could see

the twin towers, lit up like day, but there wasn't anyone inside at that hour: a manifestation of pride and power, nothing more. Man needs certitudes and illusions, I thought, and it doesn't make much difference whether they're one or the other.

Every corner on Forty-Second Street was manned by a pimp who monitored the activities of his girls without being conspicuous about it. There was one such protector—all his teeth were gold—who smiled at every pedestrian; it was, after all, his street. Another one was missing an arm, but he shook his stump vehemently and didn't feel the least bit maimed.

None of those men was particularly robust; there's no telling what violence they'd used to build their power.

Not far away, there was a group of smiling drug dealers. They moved about lazily—it wasn't as though they had to go in search of customers.

Smoke rose from the ground implacably, and it seemed as if the whole city had been plunged into hell and continued to judge me from down there. The smoke softened the gaudy brutality of the neon lights but did nothing to muffle the persistent city noises, as relentless as any eternal punishment.

I turned back uptown—when one feels this way, a little darkness is better—and one of the beauties of New York is the way everything can change in a block.

I thought about the poems I know whose themes are night, peace, quiet, and—once again—illusion. I thought about that song I love, and about its promise of pleasure. I thought about Lisa, who had moved one day closer to her end—as had we all, for that matter. I thought about her illusions and my own. And then I thought about Raj, who had been accused and sent away for something he hadn't done.

Not even the darkness could make me feel better.

All of a sudden, as I came to Fifty-Fourth Street, I heard a crowd of people who were standing at the entrance to a nightclub and shouting. A young doorman with enormous dark circles under his eyes judged who was worthy of being admitted inside, and there was nobody in the group who wasn't begging him. Getting into that place must have been really important, and they all had festive clothes on. There was a young man from out of town, accompanied by a girl he wanted to impress, but even I could see that he was out of place there, and the judge, the doorman with the big circles under his eyes, apparently deemed him unworthy of so much as a glance.

The young man wouldn't give up. It seemed to be a matter of life and death, and he was imploring the doorman, calling him by his name: "Haoui, all my friends are inside, please . . . Haoui . . ."

But the judge with the dark circles under his eyes, accustomed to better things, continued to ignore him. Suddenly the crowd burst into applause: A beautiful woman on a white horse had appeared at the end of the street and was slowly approaching across the glittering pavement.

The judge with the circles under his eyes recognized her, smiled, and asked the pestering crowd to make way for her; *she* could, without question, get in. All the noises of New York fell silent at that moment, and the only sounds you could hear on Fifty-Fourth Street were made by the white horse's triumphant hooves. And then there was renewed applause, long, ecstatic, because even the losers knew they were in the very heart of the world.

I walked away right after the woman's glorious entrance into the nightclub, while the young man continued to press his case, desperately, even though his girl was telling him, "Come on, let's go, it's not our night."

37

There are moments when life changes all of a sudden, and forever.

What we notice is the difference in rhythm, in speed, in priorities, but the reality we're reluctant to admit is that in those moments, the ultimate meaning of what happens changes, and perhaps only then can we succeed in understanding who we are.

I'd awaited Arthur's departure with anxiety; I had never missed Lisa so much. A couple of times, I'd called her up, just to hear her voice; but I remained silent, and so did she, smiling—in my imagination—just as I was. Or crying.

I'd spent the days dedicating myself with all the passion I was capable of to my work as substitute pastor, which was how I defined my status to parishioners and colleagues. And in the evening, at dinner, I'd invited Marlon and Father Lowry to discuss the challenges the world was presenting us with at that moment in time. Marlon told us that he'd been vanquished by Christ's mercy, which was the reason he'd become a priest. "That's the heart of Christianity," he added, but Father Lowry said that a Christian couldn't follow mercy alone but also justice. I seldom shared Father Olympian's ideas, but he was the person in the rectory who most wanted to engage in discussions, and for that I was grateful to him. I always avoided politics, because for one thing the subject has never fascinated me and for another Father Lowry never engaged in a political discussion without mentioning the president from Georgia with the Bible under his arm—Father L.'s unvarying description—who was weakening the country and would condemn it to great humiliations. "It's never enough just to be a good person," he always said. I don't know how true all that was, and basically it didn't interest me; our choice obligates us to deal with the heart of what generates and moves politics, even in its loftier moments. Life and death, in short, the freedom to be and therefore to define ourselves. The capacity to love, to understand, to forgive. And the duty to transmit hope. "We come before politics," I said to him one evening. "That's why, whenever we choose a flag or a side, we recognize at once how limited it is."

He didn't reply, but the two nuns smiled, as did Marlon, who then told us that one of his female parishioners had informed him that she was in a state of crisis because of the church's doctrine regarding contraception. He on the other hand embraced that doctrine, without which he wouldn't have been there at that moment. The church is mother and teacher, he added.

That was the occasion when I realized how much better my fellow priests knew the encyclicals than I did, all the encyclicals, and in particular *Humanae Vitae*. Father Olympian looked Marlon in the eye and recited the letter's opening lines from memory: "The transmission of human life is a most serious duty in which married people collaborate freely and responsibly with God the Creator . . ."

He paused for a moment and then said again, "A most serious duty." Then, without saying anything more, he stood up, bid us all a good night with only a nod of his head, and withdrew to his room.

With that, Marlon started talking about abortion and about things the world was claiming with even greater force and urgency: All those demands were essentially calls for greater freedom. He cited the *Roe v. Wade* decision and then made a reference to euthanasia; sooner or later people would be claiming that freedom too.

I said only, "Of course, exactly right," and then I excused myself in my turn, because I wanted to retire to my room and pray. Which I did at length, and without finding peace.

From the following day on, I dedicated myself with

a greater effort than ever before to the humblest and
most complicated tasks, such as fixing the boiler or
complaining to the workers at the post office, who
invariably delivered our mail a week late. To me they
seemed disorganized and incompetent, but Father
Lowry was convinced that it was some sort of anti-
Catholic boycott. Sister Beatrice and Sister Lorraine
looked at me admiringly: The parish had never been so
well organized. They hadn't been aware of that aspect
of my personality, and it was only out of respect for
Jorge that they didn't wish for me to be appointed as
his permanent replacement. The evening Father Harrigan returned we celebrated, all together, a mass of
thanksgiving: He looked quite drawn, but he was in
good humor and wanted to do all the readings himself, as a sign of humility and gratitude to the Father
who never abandons us, as he put it. Then we prayed
together for Jorge, but nobody made any allusion to
the place where he found himself at that moment.

I'd also given my best to the religious celebrations;
you can't imagine how many compliments I received
for my sermon on Saint Luke, chapter seven, the one in
which Christ is moved by the Roman centurion's insis-
tence and cures his servant. And also for my homily
on the Parable of the Prodigal Son, the most poignant
passage in the Gospels, as I told my congregation: I'd
placed them all on their guard against becoming like
that brother who set greater store by justice than by
love. And I elaborated to the point of tears upon the

father's reaction, upon his embrace, his forgiveness, his blessing. I always boast of my faith, and that's not a sin; even the liturgy says so.

On Saturday I performed a touching ceremony, the baptism of a blind infant. "What appears to us like an injustice or an atrocity follows paths known solely to the Lord, brothers and sisters in Christ. He is the way, the truth, and the life, and he is the only hope: If we follow the world's logic, nothing but ashes will remain of us, and that's the reason why today's rite asks you to renounce Satan."

I was speaking to myself, as always, thinking that the little baby I was anointing with blessed oil had a problem indeed, but it wasn't his sight, it was his soul, which was already corrupted by the original sin. And I thought that Sean Aloysius—as I had baptized him in the name of the Father, and of the Son, and of the Holy Spirit—would rejoice and suffer, like all of us. And that maybe he'd know happiness better than I did, I who decide to embrace it and to chuck it away every day of my life.

The evening Arthur left, I tried to call Lisa. There was no answer, but I refused to get agitated; she always sinks deep into unconsciousness, I thought; she's surely asleep.

I started getting worried the following morning, and by the afternoon I was overcome with anxiety when the telephone kept ringing away.

That evening I rushed over to her place with-

out even changing out of my habit, and after praying to the Lord that what I feared hadn't happened. I
knocked on her door for a long time, with desperation
in my heart. I was on the point of kicking the door
down when her next-door neighbor appeared and told
me that Miss Lisa had gone into a sudden decline and
had been transported to Bellevue Hospital. She added
that her condition was serious, very serious, as if it
were my fault.

38

Lisa had begun to feel really bad a few hours after her brother left. She'd had time to call an ambulance, but she'd decided against calling me. It was her way of protecting me, I know—her way of loving me. And of reminding us both that we're always alone. When I got to Bellevue, Arthur must still have been en route to Oregon; he couldn't have known about his sister. I thought about him in order not to think about anything else, because Lisa was lying in front of me asleep. She had an IV in one arm, and a machine was monitoring her heart, which was stubbornly resisting. The light was dim and the whole room pervaded by an acrid, nasty smell: A plastic bag that collected her urine was attached to the side of the bed.

A nurse asked me if I had brought the holy oil for anointing the sick. She was a gigantic Polish woman with brusque manners, and she frankly gave me to understand that there wasn't much time, and that I had done well to come quickly. I said no, I didn't expect this, I wasn't prepared, and then I threw my arms around her and burst into tears. The nurse freed herself from my embrace—she'd never seen such a priest—and asked me if I knew the patient well.

I limited myself to a nod, and she said the lady wasn't suffering, I could be certain of that. The cancer had spread everywhere, and her other organs were giving out; the only reason she was still alive was her strong heart.

Lisa was white, unmoving, but her body was warm, and when I kissed her forehead I could sense her feeble, raspy breath. She'd apparently had enough strength to cover her shaved head with her Maureen O'Hara wig.

I watched by her bedside all night long and then went back to the rectory at dawn. The doctor who examined Lisa had told me that her present situation might persist for a few days, maybe even a week.

And I resumed my work as if nothing was wrong, because that whole business was mine alone, unknown to all except Almighty God and a woman who had, perhaps, taken back her decision to reveal my reality to the world.

I went to see Lisa every morning right after saying mass, and I greeted her every time with a kiss on the forehead; then, after a while, I returned to my substitute pastor's duties. I missed her voice—that's what I was thinking while I consecrated the bread and wine. And her smile, which never gave way to sadness.

Then, while the divine body and blood were becoming life and hope, I looked at my unworthy hands and thought about the way she used to hug me to her before she went to sleep.

And about what she used to say to me every Sunday evening: "It would be nice if you could stay with me all day tomorrow."

I lived those days in a state of expectancy and understood that we live every moment like that.

One week later, on an afternoon suffused with weary light, there came to the rectory the last telephone call I would have expected to get.

"It's Arthur, Lisa's brother."

I couldn't say anything, and he went on: "Lisa left us two hours ago. She passed away serenely and didn't suffer."

He paused; he was a man of few words. "She loved you very much, and I know you felt the same way about her. It took me a while to realize that, and I'm making an effort not to say anything more: Lisa said that it wasn't up to me to judge."

A new pause. He'd prepared his speech, but it wasn't completely finished.

"When I was with her, she made me swear that I'd call you and ask you to celebrate her funeral mass. She said it would be the most fitting way for you to tell each other goodbye."

I didn't know what to say, but he was doing the talking.

"I'm happy to do what she wanted," he added, and he seemed sincere.

He paused yet again before saying, "She also told me to apologize to you."

I imagined his expression at that moment, and I waited uselessly for him to do his sister's bidding in this matter too. But he said no more; he couldn't go on.

39

I stared at the stained-glass windows for a long time that morning. It's the sun that gives them life, allows us to understand their meaning and their beauty. I stared at Christ's illuminated face, and I wondered why a God who loved us enough to create us needed to send his son to die on the cross to save us. Why he had left in us the mud, the failure, the pain. Why he permits evil to keep on spreading, winning, and why he insists on asking us to trust.

The redemption passes through the *via crucis*; Father John always used to remind me of that truth. But existence remains a mystery, even to those who have faith.

Lisa's parents were sitting in the first pew, a middle-aged couple whose features were devoid of all doubt. When they entered the church, they had each caressed the casket without looking at it: Inside that unadorned box, their daughter's body had begun to decay, and soon it would be eaten by worms.

I got the impression that Lisa looked like both of them: The mother had the same penetrating eyes, which I couldn't look at for long. And the father had the same cheekbones, the same coloring, the same smile. Her life had immortalized them, but then they had survived her.

Sean and Mary Kate—those were their names—had come from Oregon to take her back to where she'd been born and raised. They hadn't ever been to New York, and they still hadn't been able to understand why their daughter had chosen to live here.

Mary Kate was a tiny woman, even smaller than Lisa, but it was she who had to support her husband, who was petrified by grief. Beside them sat Arthur, dressed in a blue suit too tight for him and making a concerted effort to follow the ritual, which he barely knew: He followed the responses of the congregation a few beats late and repeated the words "We give thanks to God" even in places where the liturgy didn't call for them. He was wearing dark glasses—he didn't want his tears to be seen—and he was holding his father's arm; he knew which of them was weaker. I avoided his eyes and had trouble breathing; my broken nose, I figured.

And I said the mass with excruciating attention to

minutiae, because the sacrament is made up of details, as is the illusion, and whoever was suffering on that day had a right to both one and the other.

Nevertheless, I avoided too much solemnity, for Lisa was moderate in all things. But soon I would have to preach my homily, which she'd had her brother ask me to do: Her way of continuing to defy the world and perpetuating our sport, our love.

There couldn't have been more than twenty mourners in attendance in the church, which seemed enormous.

A small group of young people were sitting behind Lisa's parents. They must have been her college classmates—they all looked like art students. They were wearing multicolored clothes, and they had come to bid their friend a last farewell, which was something inconceivable at their age. And they did it with affection, you could tell that from their eyes, from the way they were sitting close together to give one another strength; but that ritual was a penalty they had to pay, and the readings that promised eternal life were a lie that made their farewells yet more painful. Lisa had seldom spoken to me about her friends. She didn't belong to the world that surrounded her, she used to say, and there was no environment in which she didn't feel ill at ease. So that's another reason why I'm with you, Abram, you who have refused the world.

That's not true, Lisa, I'd say, I wouldn't be here, and after that we'd talk only with our eyes.

For an instant I saw her in front of me, with her head on my shoulder, on a Sunday evening. There wasn't a time when she didn't ask me if I had said mass, if I'd taken and given Communion.

She wasn't trying to be provocative or shocking or even malicious: She wanted to understand me, to understand us, to understand what our love meant, what its limits were, what sort of future it had. And I'd always reply with a simple yes, I'd celebrated the mass, I'd taken Communion, and I'd distributed Christ's body and blood to the faithful. Yes, Lisa, yes, I said the mass because that's what a priest does, and I wasn't thinking about the future because any additional consideration caused fear and desperation.

I searched the eyes of those young people, looking for something of what she'd told me about them: There was one who knew all there was to know about Piero della Francesca, and who had tutored Lisa and courted her; it must have been that one, with the curly hair. I'd hoped that she would fall in love with him, but then I'd imagined them together and the thought had made me jealous.

And the blond girl with the glasses: She was the one Lisa had studied Fra Filippo Lippi with. I tried to recall the name of the novice who bore Lippi's son, Filippino, and when I remembered Lucrezia Buti, I almost said her name aloud.

I managed to appear calm, even detached, but I felt I was shaking, and when we all invoked the "Saint," I thought about the day I accompanied her when she went to have an abortion.

Lisa.

Lisa, my love.

Lisa, you who prayed in secret.

Lisa, you whom I didn't make a mother.

Lisa, you for whom I betrayed Christ.

Lisa, you whom I caused to live a lie.

Lisa, you whom it falls to me to bury.

Lisa, shut up in that casket, shorn of your hair.

Lisa, nothing ends forever; I must believe that.

I wondered if Arthur had children and if his parents were grandparents. I wondered how many more years they would live, Sean and Mary Kate, and how it felt to see your own future denied. Did they have faith?, I wondered. What might their sins have been, their secrets, their weaknesses, and what hopes could they still have? What could they have thought about the fact that the priest who said their daughter's funeral mass was covered with bruises and had a large bandage on his nose?

Only then did I notice that among the occupants of the last pew were Sister Beatrice and Sister Lorraine. Maybe they were telling me something, or maybe not; maybe they simply wanted to say farewell to a young woman who had sacrificed her own time to help the homeless: The Lord would reward her.

And that was what I talked about in my sermon; in her brief life, I said, Lisa had known how to love. And now this young sister in Christ had returned to her Father's house. That's the way we express ourselves, we priests.

I described how Lisa had explained to me the beauty of the Scrovegni Chapel. "The purest things often spring from our weaknesses, from our disgraces, brothers and sisters. From our weaknesses," I said again, and then I added, "And I thank you, Lisa, I thank you," but I wasn't able to say anything else.

I had the impression that of all the people in the church, only Sister Beatrice and Sister Lorraine had faith, but I went on because I was talking to Lisa, to me, to both of us, and I was defying Almighty God once again; that was what she'd asked me to do for the last time.

At that moment there was a big party in heaven, I said, because this young sister of ours had awakened from the dream of life. But in reality, I was praying that I too would obtain the grace to awaken from that dream.

"Welcome her, Heavenly Father, you who know our hearts and our misfortunes."

The curly-haired young man looked at me perplexed, but I wasn't discouraged.

"Welcome her, you who have given us our corrupt bodies."

I said a third and then a fourth time, "Welcome her," and then I don't know how many more, before bursting into tears when I asked Lisa to pray for us who remained in this land of illusions, this world that you, Heavenly Father, are able to love.

"Welcome her."

I was silent for a long time, the tears running down my face, and the few people who had gathered in that church thought that the death of someone so young had devastated even a priest, who must have seen so many deaths.

"Welcome her."

I saw what was left of Lisa for the last time on the parvis in front of the church. The funeral home would take charge of her cremation before consigning her ashes to her parents.

The colorfully clothed young people, all together, sang "Bridge Over Troubled Water" and then bade farewell to Lisa one by one, saying simply, "So long, Lisa." They too had a rite to perform.

I imagined her with them and wondered why she didn't feel that she was part of them—they seemed so affectionate.

I hugged Sean and Mary Kate hard, and they were moved and embraced me too: They hadn't expected a priest to feel so much affection for their daughter.

At that point I hugged Arthur too, who neither mingled with the young people nor took off his dark glasses. He remained silent, and then as I was walking away, he said softly, "I apologize." And I shut my eyes, because it was another thing I wanted to keep to myself.

Lisa's fellow students went off toward the bar across from the church: The day was too beautiful, and the curly-haired lad promised to buy everyone a round of beer.

While they were leaving, Father Lowry informed me that the boiler was broken again, and he suffered a lot from the cold.

Yes, it was a dazzlingly bright day, a brazen day, and I replied that I would surely see about the boiler. As we were going back into the church, Sister Lorraine promised to cook oven-roasted potatoes, a dish I'd always loved, for dinner; I didn't have to feel alone that evening.

40

The prayer I said every day was a request that I would no longer be a symbol, a reference point. That I wouldn't be forgotten. But the prayer was wrong, as I well knew.

As soon as I returned to the rectory, I notified Jorge that I wanted to go away. "Like Andrew, my fellow seminarian. And like many other brothers who have devoted their lives to those who suffer. If the Lord has given me any talent, it's not in the words I speak from the altar, it's in my actions: I've worked on buildings a hundred stories tall, defying and glorifying heaven."

And Jorge smiled at my arrogance: He knows the world because he knows pain. He'd lost a lot of weight, but I'd never seen him so strong in spirit, so alert. He said he'd talk to the bishop about my request; in the meantime, however, I would have to continue to perform my everyday duties. "We do good even against our will, Abram, and even when we don't know it."

After our conversation, I went into the church. All the lights had been turned off, and I tried to pray. I can never find the words when I need them, and the only thing I kept thinking about was the question of whether death was light or darkness. Inside the church, there were only a few candles burning.

The moment when I made my choice crossed my mind, the moment when I prostrated myself before the altar. How many congratulations I had received that evening! I'd become a model to be emulated; the world seemed happy to celebrate someone who had chosen not to be a part of it. And at that moment I was ready to challenge it—the world—and to defeat it, because I was certain I could defeat myself. I remembered the aroma of the incense, the Latin words that made me feel part of an eternal story, and the bells, ringing out in jubilation because among the many who had been called, one had been chosen, one had followed the right path.

Si vis perfectus esse.

How far off that goal is now. But how lovely it was to dream of it, to desire it.

Even strength is a mirage, I thought, and so are promises, choices, even courage: All we can do is learn to be less weak. And to grow less attached to our weaknesses.

I wonder what my father would say about me. I

wonder why our Heavenly Father didn't want me to know my own. And why he didn't want my father to be by my side whenever I needed him. I wonder what the woman who wanted to denounce me would say at this point. I wonder why she hasn't turned me in. I wonder if she ever will. I wonder what my uncle Nicola, horrified as he was by my decision to renounce the world, would say now: He'd smile, probably, because I have remained most thoroughly in the world. Or maybe not, because this world is scary as well, and maybe, deep down inside, he'd like to renounce it too. And I wonder what my mother would say, she who needs neither a habit nor promises to have a dialogue with God. And Father John, and Andrew, and Luis, who had lost the love of his life. And the lady in the Amish country who thought I was a rabbi.

In the back of the church, in the pew where the homeless sometimes lie down, Father Harrigan was sitting, and he was having no difficulty praying. Bobbing his head slightly, he talked directly to the tabernacle. He'd recovered, but he was well aware that he didn't have much time left: a year, maybe two, or maybe much less, a few weeks, a few days. He seemed, however, neither frightened nor resigned; tired, if anything, and in fact, after a short while, he began to snore.

I left without making any noise; I didn't want to wake him. I stared at the dark stained-glass windows.

Later, in bed, I imagined myself in the mud-walled

stilt huts on the outskirts of Manila and in the rust-and-aluminum shacks of Johannesburg. And then in a cold desert, where no one had ever heard of Christ. I felt a need to humble myself, to obliterate myself. To flay myself: My body should serve only to do good to others. I prayed to be sent to the most destitute place in the world, and to have the strength and simplicity of Andrew, whom I had admired and forgotten as I do everything that compels me to look in the mirror. I wanted to feel the weight of life on my flesh: I was spoiled and full of vices and nothing else, inadequate to cope with the reality of our littleness, of our frailty.

The greatest destitution is the destitution of the soul. As I pondered that truth, which I've always known, I thought of Lisa, who had been reduced to ashes before me: She would have laughed at these fantasies of mine.

"You're a romantic," she often told me, "and you've always denied it." And I wouldn't say a word, because she knew all my defenses.

It was Sunday evening—I realized it only then—and someone, somewhere, was watching *The Honeymooners*.

That your joy may be full, I thought; the Gospels help you and frighten you. And I've been searching for that joy ever since I was born, but I've actually caught hold of it for only a few moments: when I felt I was doing good, and when I betrayed the promises I made. If God is a mystery, so too is happiness, and I've never hated him, the Heavenly Father who created me, so much. And I've never felt a greater need to beg his forgiveness.

I couldn't get to sleep that night, and at six in the morning I broke the bread and poured the wine: Our community entrusted the work of salvation to me. And at the end of the mass, Sister Lorraine and Sister Beatrice blissfully sang "The King of Love My Shepherd Is."

That day I took a long, aimless walk. Eventually I reached midtown and headed east on Fifty-Seventh Street, all the way to the river. I sat on a bench and stayed there until evening, waiting for the lights of the Queensboro Bridge to come on. It happens suddenly, when the sky isn't yet dark, and the water of the East River assiduously refracts the lights on its way to the sea: It's a spectacle that has always moved me because it's produced not for pleasure but by necessity. And it makes me see why I love this city of solitary, energetic people.

Jorge didn't talk to the bishop, and even though he would probably have listened to me, I didn't either. And after a few weeks passed, I realized that I never would.

I was put in charge of the umpteenth boiler repair, and one day Jorge called me into his office to tell me that if we were to raise the price of candles to thirty cents apiece, we'd make enough to pay the whole cost of installing the Nativity scene, and there would even be something left over to put toward repairing the organ.

I told him I thought that was a good idea. We should announce it during the masses, I said; our parishioners would be happy to make that little sacrifice.

He asked me to remain personally in charge of the parish administration—I had done such a fine job in his absence, he said. Then he suddenly changed his tone and said he had to speak to me about a matter that had been on his mind for a long time: He wanted me to celebrate his funeral mass, or more precisely, he wanted me to promise to do so. "In all probability, I'll pass away before you do," he said, adding, with a smile, "and they tell me you're good at funerals too."

I figured he must be sixty years old, maybe a little older, but he was neither elderly nor sick: No telling why he was thinking about death, and no telling what he saw in me. The current rumor was that he'd started drinking again and that he was hiding wine behind the big Bible in his library, but that was just some evil-tongued parishioners' gossip: He seemed perfectly sober to me.

"We all need young priests like you," he concluded. "Priests immersed in the world."

I thought that life is full of irony, even more than mystery, and I gave him my word with a smile, unable to add anything more. Then, that very evening, I began to devote my attention to the parish accounts, and at the end of every mass I explained the reason for the rise in the price of candles.

I've spoken no more to Jorge about my desire to

go away, and I've often gone with him to visit Blanca, the little Ecuadorean girl. We never speak during those visits, but we return home through the park, where he describes to me the provenance of every tree. We clamber over the granite rocks as if we were out in the country, and then we lose ourselves in wonder at what man has built around that enormous garden, whose plants come from every part of the world. Once he pointed out a hawks' nest on the roof of a Fifth Avenue building. "This city is still wild," was his only comment. But then he added, "And that's its appeal."

Then one day, all of a sudden, he asked me to call Raj back. "It wasn't him, Abram, and we have to apologize to him." He didn't add anything else, there was no need to, and I for my part had been rendered speechless, but that evening, right after dinner, he did some talking for a change, and he quoted a meditation he always returned to, a proposition stated by one of the Desert Fathers: "Both God and the Evil One want you to become a saint. Only the devil wants you to become one right away."

We all fell silent until Sister Beatrice got up to clear the table and I instinctively followed her.

Then, the next morning, when Raj came back to resume making sandwiches for the homeless, I knelt down before him for all to see. The poor Indian boy couldn't understand the meaning of my gesture.

That day I felt trepidation at all I had done and then suppressed: I asked myself when I would find the strength to atone. God is merciful, I know, and it may be that my littleness deserves laughter and nothing else, but the role I've chosen to interpret is more important than I am.

A few weeks later, I felt a new desire, hot and strong, for a woman who came to make her confession. Nina was her name, and during the evening mass I couldn't drive a fantasy image of her naked body out of my mind.

I had dinner with Jorge, the nuns, and the old priests. Marlon suggested we see some movies together, he and I; we have to understand how the world expresses itself, he said. A couple of films about the war in Vietnam have come out, and we decided to see them in the following days.

After we finished dinner, Sister Beatrice switched on the television. It was quiz-show night. I stayed and watched for a little while, and then, before retiring to my room, I thanked the Lord for my frailties, my desires, and my fears, which remind me that I'm a man. And I thanked him for my shame, which has never disappeared; that too is a grace.

Later that night, in the solitude of my cheerless room, I got down on my knees, knowing that I would fall again. And again.

And then I tried to sleep, defying the sleepless city.

Acknowledgments

On this occasion more than on any other, I feel obligated to thank, first of all, my brother Andrea, who followed with intelligence, respect, and passion every step in the writing of this novel. My gratitude grows even warmer if I think about Andrea's sunny disposition, so distant from the character whose story I've undertaken to tell.

I want to express my thanks to all my friends at Mondadori, who continue to believe in me and in this project, my New York saga: Gianni Ferrari, first and foremost, because of whom I became a writer. And then Carlo Carabba, Mario de Laurentiis, Francesco Anzelmo, Francesca Gariazzo, Cristiano Moroni, Mara Samaritani, Nadia Focile, and Monica Gambera. I'd also like to add Antonio Franchini and Giulia Ichino, who followed the first stages of this book: I've made the most of some precious words of advice they gave me concerning that initial work, and I want to tell Antonio that we will surely have an opportunity to talk some more about boxing.

Affectionate thanks to everyone at the Wylie Agency who supported me with their usual dedication, especially Andrew, Sarah, and Rebecca.

I also warmly acknowledge a debt of gratitude to my friends from forever: Davide, Ginevra, Marina, and Stefano. What I'm particularly grateful to you for is your seriousness that never becomes gravity, and the smiles with which you remind me that it takes lightness to reach the depths.

This is the place to admit that in my depiction of Jorge's life, there's an idea stolen from Ernest Hemingway: This appropriation is my way of paying homage to a magnificent story, which has stayed with me ever since the first time I read it. I also wish to extend my gratitude to Patti Smith for permission to use lyrics from her song "Because the Night."

And I send a warm embrace to all my family, in Italy and in New York. The thing I mostly have in common with Abram is his fear of solitude, and it's your love that lets me overcome that fear: You're my port of departure and my port of arrival. To Marilù, Caterina, Ignazio, and Jacquie, I want to say that you all are my strength. And my happiness.

A Note About the Author

Antonio Monda is the author of five novels and five collections of essays. His books have been translated into eleven languages. He is a regular contributor to *La Repubblica*, and his work has also appeared in *The Paris Review, Fiction, The Common,* and *Vanity Fair*. He lives in New York City, where he teaches at New York University.

A Note About the Type

The text of this book was set in Sabon, a typeface designed by Jan Tschichold (1902–1974), the well-known German typographer.